LOVE IN CENTRAL AMERICA

ALSO BY CLANCY MARTIN

Love and Lies
How to Sell
Introducing Philosophy
The German Sisyphus
The Philosophy of Deception
Ethics Across the Professions
Honest Work
Since Socrates
Morality and the Good Life
Above the Bottom Line

LOVE IN CENTRAL AMERICA

CLANCY MARTIN

Harvill *Secker*

LONDON

1 3 5 7 9 10 8 6 4 2

Harvill Secker, an imprint of Vintage,
20 Vauxhall Bridge Road,
London SW1V 2SA

Harvill Secker is part of the Penguin Random House
group of companies whose addresses can be found at
global.penguinrandomhouse.com

Penguin
Random House
UK

First published by Harvill Secker in 2016
First published with the title *Bad Sex* in 2015
by Tyrant Books, New York

penguin.co.uk/vintage

A CIP catalogue record for this book is available from the
British Library

ISBN 9781846559587

Printed and bound in Great Britain by Clays Ltd, St Ives PLC

Penguin Random House is committed to a sustainable future
for our business, our readers and our planet. This book is made
from Forest Stewardship Council® certified paper.

MIX
Paper from
responsible sources
FSC
www.fsc.org   FSC® C018179

For ZC

Thank you for never giving up

"This wasn't invented, it really happened"
– Alejandro Zambra

ONE

ONE OF US HAD TO WATCH OUR HOTEL IN TULUM during the storm, so I was flying into Cancun International then renting a car. The hurricane had closed all of the airports on the coast, and my flight was delayed, and then cancelled. As I was walking out of the airport, I heard an announcement my flight was boarding. It was the last flight into Cancun. When I got to the hotel, I told the story to the clerk and she laughed and upgraded me to a suite. "It will just sit empty anyway," she told me, as though she were apologizing for the change. "We're getting flooded with cancellations." I asked her for an envelope, put sixty dollars into it, and handed it back to her. The room was enormous, with a dining room table, a kitchen in case you'd brought your own cook, and floor-to-ceiling windows with long views of the ocean. The waves were huge and confused in the storm, and they stretched as far as I could see in the rain.

It was ten in the morning.

TWO

I PACED AROUND THE ROOM, LOOKED AT MYSELF IN
the mirror, went to the bathroom, and then opened
my computer on the desk. I sat for a few minutes, trying to tell myself I could write, and then moved to the
bed and read the room service menu. When I came
to the wine list in the back, I closed it. I went over
to the window, leaned my forehead against the cold
glass, and stared down the ten stories. My forehead
made a smear on the glass. I got a Coke Light from
the minibar. Then I took off my shoes and jacket and
sat on the couch to call Paul.

"I'm already lonely for you," I said. It was the day after Christmas, and the truth was I was glad for a break. Paul's boys had been out of school for a week and his family had visited for the holidays. His mother was a friend of mine but she had a way of taking over the house. She was a devoted grandmother but the boys were nervous around her, because she was wealthy and uptight and dressed carefully each morning. Paul's father was there now—his parents were divorced—and he was clingy and demanding. He frequently needed to go to the pharmacy or the grocery store to buy things. But he hated Mexico City—they were from a small town in Massachusetts—and he'd get lost if he drove himself. He was good with the boys but he liked to tell us how to parent them. Also, after a few days Paul felt like he had a third child in the house.

"My dad is driving me crazy. He keeps getting angry when I won't stay up and watch a movie with him. We watched two Burt Reynolds movies last night and he wasn't satisfied. Hurry home," he said. "I need you here right now."

"I'm sorry. One of us had to go. It's three nights. I really ought to be here for at least a week. And I've already got a little writing done. It's so quiet here, with the hurricane, there's nothing else to do. I'll drive down to Tulum tomorrow or the next day."

"Don't get on the road until the weather is better. You're writing? That's good. I told you. How's the Ritz?"

"It hasn't changed. Anyway, without you, it's a room. It doesn't matter."

We didn't have anything to talk about but I didn't want him to get off the phone.

THREE

I CALLED MY FRIEND SADIE, A DOCTOR FROM GALVES-
ton, Texas. I hadn't seen her in a couple of years, and
she was driving to Cancun to meet me for the weekend. She wasn't afraid of the storm.

I hadn't told Paul that Sadie was coming. Not for
any reason. I knew it would annoy him. It was understood that this was a necessary but unfortunate work
trip that one of us had to make and since they were
his boys I was the one going, and I wasn't supposed to
enjoy myself. But I should have told him I'd invited
Sadie down. He had never been crazy about Sadie.

"She's trouble," he always said about her. "All psychiatrists are crazy. But she's not just ordinary crazy. She's crazy about sex. She tries to sleep with me every time she visits."

"Paul, she does not." Maybe she did, a little. But she didn't mean anything by it.

"Man! These roads are for shit. I'd turn around right now if it weren't for you."

"I'm glad you're coming. Thanks. You want to go to Pobrecito's? I'll make a reservation."

"You're buying. Hell, I'm almost in town, I'll come to your hotel. No, you're not invited, buddy, sorry. I'm dropping you off the minute we cross the border, like you said. Del la What? That on the coast?"

"What?" I had no idea what she was talking about. "That's where they catch those green lobsters, right?"

"Tell me you didn't pick up a hitchhiker, Sadie."

"I have you on the speakerphone, Brett, watch what you say." I heard her pick up the phone. "He's a college kid. No? Well, what's with the bandana? You want any of this? Okay, fine. Well, just hold it, would ya? It's a pipe, buddy, it don't bite."

"Sadie, I gotta go."

"Can you believe this rain? Beautiful, actually. All the colors."

"Sadie, you're stoned. I'll see you when you get here. Just valet under my name."

"You just called. Alright, fine. Set up that restaurant."

I thought about calling Paul back but I knew he was busy with his dad and the boys. I needed to work. Before I started, I checked my email. Three emails from an Italian publisher panicking about a manuscript I had promised him for months. Dozens of emails from *Fab*, *Dwell*, and *Tablet*. A request to blurb a book. Fan mail. An invitation to sit on someone's doctoral dissertation. I started to switch into Word when I saw there was one from Paul's banker. "I'm in Cancun," was the header. "Do you have time for a cup of coffee today or tonight? Paul said you're here. I was supposed to be in Panama, but I'm stuck with everybody else. They say I'll get a flight tomorrow. Yrs, Eduard."

Eduard and I had met briefly once at a party nearly a decade before, but I didn't remember it. I only knew because Paul told me so.

"He's not the kind of man you would notice," Paul said. "He's old, a bit chubby, and he doesn't know how to dress."

I didn't want to meet with Eduard but thought I probably should.

Plus, now if I met Eduard, Paul would find out Sadie was in Cancun.

•

I wrote to Eduard. "I have a friend in town from Texas, a psychiatrist I've known since high school, but if you want to meet us, it would be great. I'd love to hang out. What's a good bar? You'd be doing me a favor, in fact. My friend Sadie is a drinker, and this way she'll have a drinking buddy."

Eduard wrote back immediately: "I don't know the bars in Cancun. I'll try to find a place close to your hotel. Paul said you're at the Ritz-Carlton?"

FOUR

SADIE CAME UP TO MY ROOM AROUND SIX.

"Wow, look at this place. I should have just stayed with you."

"That's what I said. You can. Cancel your room."

"No, you know me. I sometimes stay up late." She laughed. I could see she was still stoned. "I'm going to make a drink. You want a club soda?"

I told her the news.

"Man, I thought it was going to be girls' night out," she said. "What about that horse place we were planning on? I want to see those horses. Cowboys!

Mexican cowboys are still the real thing. I thought we had reservations."

"Oh, I changed it to tomorrow. This won't take long. We'll have one drink with him, then we can hit the town. Wherever you want to go."

"Boring. You've been doing this to me for twenty-five years. Always some man."

"I've been doing it to you? Please. He's not a man, Sadie. He's Paul's banker."

Sadie rolled her eyes.

"Those days are behind me. We're old women. We're practically middle-aged."

"Speak for yourself," Sadie said. She was two years younger than me.

FIVE

EDUARD HAD PICKED AN EXPENSIVE BAR IN A BASE-
ment in the old town. It took the taxi almost an hour
to find the place. It was packed. The ceilings were
low and the zinc bar stretched the entire length of
the room. It was lit with dozens of bare Edison bulbs,
and on the back wall they had glass cabinets filled
with taxidermy molds and instruments. They'd have
to redo the whole place in two years, I thought. New
Mexico in old Cancun.

"This place is cool," Sadie said. "This is like a bar in New York. You wouldn't even know where you were if it weren't for all the Mexicans."

Sadie had red hair. She had freckles on the bridge of her nose, and was slender with extraordinary legs and excellent posture. She was pretty in a way that made women hate and worship her.

I ordered her a martini and watched the door for Eduard. I was worried I wouldn't recognize him—I had no picture in my mind at all—and so I stared at all the men who came and went. An hour passed. Sadie told me a long story about one of her patients who was emotionally abusive to her husband. After three years of treatment, the woman broke down and confessed that she was not married.

"Now that's a woman who's fucking crazy," she said. "No better word for her. What the hell am I supposed to do with this woman? She still comes to see me. There's a novel in that one for you. You can use it to break your slump."

I said, "Maybe you should write it."

I wondered if I could have gotten the night wrong. I checked my email on my phone.

"Where the hell is he? I thought a banker worked for you, not the other way around. I'm hungry. What time did he say?"

"Nine."

"Shit, it's quarter after ten, and we haven't had any dinner. I'm starving. I'm getting a hamburger. Do you want a burger? Rare?"

Sadie got a hamburger, and her third double martini. I ordered things I thought Eduard might like, things that wouldn't go cold: olives, cheese, salami, roasted peppers, anchovies, lobster. The bartender recommended the truffle fries so I got those too.

"And one more Coke Light, if you don't mind. Sorry. I drink these things like water."

"You know those are bad for you," the bartender said. He smiled. "Poison. Let me make you a ginger ale. Trust me. Do you like eucalyptus?"

I shrugged, and he turned to start on my drink.

SIX

"MAN THAT BARTENDER IS HOT," SADIE SAID. IT WAS noisy but she said it loud enough for him to hear. "He totally hit on you. Did you see that?" She raised her voice. "It's funny because I'm the one who's interested. In him." The bartender turned and looked at her. "You," she said, and raised her drink.

Sadie's husband was wealthy. He was handsome and young, but she had never been in love with him. She was happy in her marriage, but slept with other men. "Hell, he knows," she always said. "But he doesn't know what he doesn't want to know, and I can keep my mouth shut."

Paul had asked me to make a similar promise when we first started dating. "Life is long, and you may cheat on me one day," he said. "If you do, just promise me you won't tell me about it."

"I'll never cheat on you," I said, but still I promised. I never had. "This is a great burger," Sadie said. "You should have a burger. I'm gonna have another one. They're so tiny it's like a slider. In Galveston they'd serve you three of these."

"I guess I'll get one too," I said.

They had a clothing rack at the bottom of the stairs and a man was taking off a white windbreaker. He hung it on a hanger. He was wearing weird black leather gloves, and he took time getting them off his hands and into his coat pockets. That can't be him, I thought. He was dressed stylishly. He wore a black suit. The pants were tailored tight to his legs. He had a grey shirt on and a narrow grey tie. Contrary to what Paul said, he had hair. It was cut short, but growing long. He smiled and waved.

"Man, is that him?" Sadie said. "Tell me that's him. That's not a banker. That's a fuckmaster prince."

"I don't know what you are talking about." I stood to meet him.

"Seriously," Sadie was saying. "He looks like Benicio Del Toro."

Eduard walked up quickly and I held out my hand. He pushed it aside, hugged me, and gave me a kiss on the cheek. His lips were cold from outside. He took a seat at the bar.

"You know what? You look like a movie star," Sadie said. "Brett said you were like an ordinary man. I mean—you don't look like a banker."

"Brett said I was ordinary?"

He winked at me and ordered a whiskey.

"Make it a double," I said to the bartender, leaning forward so Sadie and Eduard wouldn't hear. "And water down her martini a bit."

"Your husband?" the bartender asked.

"Oh, he's not my husband. He's my husband's banker." The bartender laughed, and I ordered another ginger ale.

SEVEN

WE TALKED, THEY KEPT DRINKING, AND SADIE AND
Eduard seemed to be hitting it off. Occasionally Eduard's legs bumped against mine. At first I didn't think
it was intentional. The bar was getting too crowded.

"Would you like a hamburger?" I asked Eduard.
"Sadie says they're good."

"The burgers?" Sadie yelled. "They're great! The
burgers are great. Brett, do you think they have buf-
falo wings? Eduard, how about you and me split a
dozen wings? And chips and salsa! How come Mexico
is the only place you can't get chips and salsa?"

"I'm sorry. Our kitchen is closed," the bartender said. He had just served a final round of drinks.

"We'll take two burgers and a dozen wings!" Sadie said. "Those are great burgers. Delicious! Where'd you get the cows?"

"Apparently we need some food," I said to the bartender.

"If you go two blocks toward the water there's a place. Also, there's the Dino hotel, and they serve good pizza."

Eduard took me by the wrist. "Doesn't pizza sound fantastic? Hawaiian pizza, that's what I want." He swallowed half of his drink, paused, and then swallowed the other half. Sadie was almost at the bottom of her martini. I had lost track of their drinks. I'd had four or five ginger ales.

"Yeah, pizza!" Sadie said. She grabbed Eduard around the waist. He put one arm around her shoulders, and lay the other on mine. He was almost a foot taller than either of us. I could have fit under his chin.

"You're drunk," I said.

For an hour or so, I had been worried because I thought, if he is flirting with me, I'm enjoying it. But now I decided it was alright. He was flirting with both of us, but it was innocent.

"Let's go, let's go," Sadie said. It was pouring rain. We walked up the cobble-stoned street, swaying and laughing, getting soaked. "Pizza man!" Sadie shouted. "Pizza man! Hey put that dog on a leash!"

A woman and man walking under a giant umbrella turned to look at us, startled. Sadie pointed across the street to an old, distinguished looking man in a yellow raincoat and wide-brimmed hat, and his wet, carefully-groomed white poodle. The dog was walking beside him and they both seemed not to notice the rain. Three tough-looking guys on the corner stood under a tattered awning, watching us. They had beers in their hands. Sadie slipped on a heel and Eduard caught her and almost fell, pulling me down as well. The three men laughed, and I saw it was okay.

But the restaurant at the hotel was closed, and so was the little place across the street with bars on the windows. All of the garage doors were pulled down across the businesses, the streets were empty except for us and the billboards for concrete companies and auto part stores, and I thought, "Maybe they will go home together. How am I going to get a car?"

Eduard said. "What about your hotel? Or mine? You're at the Ritz-Carleton, right? It must have a restaurant. You're the hotel expert."

"It's half an hour from here," I said. "If we can find a cab."

"I've got my car," Eduard said.

"She's got the Presidential suite!" Sadie said. "I'm staying there too. But her room is like a palace. And it's got this oversize minibar too, so you can eat all you want. You can eat anything! Plus, free booze!"

"Sound good?" Eduard asked me.

I thought, well, they'll eat, and then they'll go to bed.

EIGHT

EDUARD AND I WERE SITTING ON THE RED LEATHER
sofa and Sadie was in the chair next to the minibar.
They had finished their steaks and were picking at
their salads. I was exhausted. Sadie didn't want to
leave, and Eduard was still talking and drinking. They
both had booze energy. The party's over, I thought. I
went to the bathroom and saw that Paul had called
six times. He does not have a cell phone—he hates
technology—and so I didn't return his call: I didn't
like to imagine our home phones waking up his boys,

and particularly Paul's father, who, when he had been drinking, would crawl into Paul's bed in his pajamas.

When I sat down Sadie opened the minibar again. She reached across Eduard's lap to refill his drink, allowing her shirt to fall open. She looked up at him and dropped her hand onto his leg. Eduard stood suddenly and went to the bathroom.

Sadie sat upright. She said, "I think I'll go down to my room."

"Please," I said, "it's late. Just stay here in my place tonight." She gave me an angry look.

"Sadie," I said, "this is ridiculous. There's three bedrooms in this suite, I think. Or just sleep in bed with me."

At that point I still meant everything I was saying. At least, I'm pretty sure I did.

She was already walking to the door. She stopped, turned, and looked at me for a moment when I said that, and I realized she was furious. I let her go. I sat and watched the ice melting in Eduard's whiskey and Sadie's vodka and almost picked one of them up to finish it. Then I realized, that's how tired you are. It had been two years, almost to the day, since I'd had a drink.

Eduard came out of the bathroom. "Sadie left?"

"Yes. Jesus Christ. I'm sorry. I didn't expect her to get so drunk. We didn't get to talk. You're flying out tomorrow?"

"I think so," he said. "Who knows." He put more ice in his drink and gestured at the window. The rain was going sideways. Up the beach in the lights from another resort you could see the palm trees bending almost to the ground. "Don't you want one?" he asked.

"One what?" I knew what he meant.

"A drink. I don't care if you have one. Have one." His smile was unexpected. He knew about my alcoholism. He said he'd read my novel, and even if he hadn't, in the old days Paul had loved to complain to his friends about my drinking. I hesitated.

"Don't ever offer me a drink," I said. "I mean, I can't."

"I just thought, you know, one. It doesn't do any harm."

"Yeah," I said. I didn't say anything else about that.

He took a couple sips of his drink and asked, "Do you want to watch a movie?"

He got up and walked into the bedroom, where the TV was. From there he said, "It's cold in here. Let's get under the covers."

You always want a man to say that to you but they never do. When I'd stopped drinking I stopped behaving this way and I thought it was behind me. As I got into bed with him, I was still thinking, this is not the kind of thing that I do. He took the back of my head with one hand, and my throat and the base of my chin with the other. He kissed me.

When we stopped kissing, a long time later, I said, "Eduard, I'm happily married."

"I know," he said.

We had sex until dawn. The storm had blown south and the sun was over the sea. We had sex at least seven times. An hour or so into it he told me that his girlfriend didn't like sex, and I was determined to make an impression.

NINE

"It's only three nights, Brett. He's our lifeline. We need him."

"No, that's not what I'm saying. I want to meet him. I'm glad he's coming. I understand. It's just that I am barely back from Cancun. And now you've invited a friend to stay. Not a friend. Your banker."

"Brett, it's not like I called him up. He has an appointment in town with Sergio."

Sergio was one of Eduard's partners, and he handled all of our personal banking. He actually looked like I remembered Eduard looking.

"It's business. I don't want him to stay in a hotel. It'd be different if we had a property here. It's only polite."

"Right."

"Can I ask you, what is your problem with Eduard?"

"I don't have any problem, it just seems a bit odd to have him staying in our home. Did he ask to stay with us?"

Eduard and I had been talking on the phone almost every night. He texted me during the day. We wrote long emails.

It had snuck up on me. He'd come down to our hotel in Tulum after the weekend with Sadie in Cancun.

It should have been a one-night thing, but we had both become fanatical at the same time. I was amazed at my own weakness.

"I told you. I invited him to stay here."

"A week?"

"I couldn't exactly tell him how long he's allowed to stay."

"Your dad's going to be in town at the same time. It's not going to be very nice for him. He wants all of us to spend time together."

"My dad can't expect us to drop everything every time he comes to town. He doesn't expect us to."

"Whatever. I'm just asking for a bit of help."

"You're asking for a bit of help."

"I don't like your tone, Paul."

"I've had the kids all by myself for weeks, and you don't like my tone."

I didn't remind him that the whole time I'd been gone, I was checking on our hotels. I didn't say he'd had Bella, his mom and his eldest son helping him, but I thought it. The more in the wrong I was, the easier it was for me to feel indignant. But I knew I was not in a position of leverage.

And of course I wanted Eduard to stay at our house.

"You're supposed to be off work for at least a few days. It's Christmas. I don't know why he has to come during the holiday. It's just not considerate."

"I don't set his schedule, Brett. Jesus. You know the position we're in. This is all part of expanding our properties. I mean, we're a bit stretched, honestly. The last thing we need to do right now is piss off the money guys."

We had bought several hotels in resort locations a year before—some in excellent condition, some a mess—and we were still deep in renovations on a big place in Guatemala and a beachfront place in Panama. Paul's family had lots of money, but Paul had to make his own living, naturally.

"We have plenty of money," I said. "We can live on the income from your trusts if we just turn over Los Imperealos. Just sell it as is. Or let's have a party and bring some private people in. That's what your mom did. She always says private investors are the only good investors. Let's find a few angels."

"I'm not ready for this fight again," Paul said. "I promise while he's in town I will make time to be home. I wish he weren't coming. Nobody wishes that more than I do. And Bella can take care of all the meals—or we'll go out."

"No," I said, "have it your way, Paul. If he's coming, he's coming. We'll do it properly."

TEN

I'D LIVED IN MEXICO FOR TWELVE YEARS, BUT I HAD never made love to a Mexican man before. Most of the other ex-pats of a certain age had affairs with young Mexican men and I thought it was obvious and humiliating. "Toreador," Viola called hers; Becky's nickname for her current was "Rabbit." I tried "The Goat" on Eduard but it never stuck. His name was always Eduard. His features were masculine: he had rough skin around his cheeks, his shoulders were wide but round, and he was not muscled but he was beautifully shaped and he was tall. He had been a boxer when he was in high school and college, and sometimes he'd stand on the bed and use my arms from behind to show me how to throw punches. He was awkward though and I knew many of my friends would be surprised if they knew. On the outside there was something about the two of us, if you looked at us, that didn't quite fit. But he would stop in windows and hold me and say: "Now that's a beautiful couple" or "Look at the young lovers" and kiss me. He could hold me by the back of the neck and toss me like a puppy. When he wore one of his suits and it was the cocktail hour and he took his first drink, my stomach turned, even after I knew him a year.

We could talk on the phone for five hours. One morning we started talking at just after eight and didn't get off the phone until he had to go home at six my time. He asked unexpected questions that made me see everything from a perspective that I had not imagined before. It sounds insincere, but he worried about Paul and the boys. One night, on the phone with him, in the car on the way back from the grocery store, I broke down crying and said, "I'm a terrible wife. I'm not a good person. I'm as bad as everyone says." He said, "Don't flatter yourself. You're no better and no worse than anyone else."

Sometimes, after we'd had an argument, he'd leave the hotel room and come back with a cut cheek, bruised ribs or a split lip. He was a grown man but he'd go get in a street brawl, in his suit and tie. I was

never physically afraid of him. He was the most intimate lover I've ever had. "I listen to you," he'd tell
me, when I asked him how he knew to do the things
he did.

ELEVEN

HE DIDN'T BELIEVE ME WHEN I TOLD HIM I HAD A past.

"Well, I won't let you read my new book," I said. It was a book I had been working on for five years, and would never finish. "You'll think I slept with half of New York, and every able-bodied cowboy in Texas. Of course those were my drinking days. Most of that was before I met Paul. I mean it was all before Paul. Or before Paul and I were serious. There was one guy, a lawyer. I forget his name. This was a decade ago. He was a friend of Paul's. We were out at lunch, and when Paul left the table, I told him we should have a French affair. I suggested we meet in the afternoons for sex."

"Sounds like a good deal for him." Eduard didn't like to hear about my former lovers. But I didn't care. It wasn't a casual affair and I wanted him to know me.

"He wanted to meet at his apartment. He was too cheap to pay for a hotel. I stood outside of his building for nearly an hour, sweating in the sun, wearing a new dress and these stupid Chanel sunglasses—"

"I love those sunglasses."

"Well, I finally called him. He didn't answer. Then I got a text message. It said, 'I forgot this is my laundry day. I only get one day a week to do laundry. Maybe next week?'"

"I don't believe you."

"That was the text. Word for word."

"Did you meet with him the next week?" I bit him on the shoulder.

"You honestly think I would meet with him after that?"

"I don't even know why I'm asking. I don't want to know."

"He was astonishing. He had a whole toolbox. It was better than a porn movie." I said it with a straight face. The truth was I'd introduced that guy to You-Porn and RedTube. It took me a while to convince Eduard I was joking.

I said, "All women over twenty-seven are whores."
Of course I might have just been talking about myself.

TWELVE

I WAS CHUBBY AS A KID. MY MOTHER TOLD ME, "DON'T worry, your time will come." Once, on an airplane, flying to Copenhagen where my grandmother is from, a handsome man sitting beside me spread a blanket across my legs and his own. My mom was asleep right next to me. Everyone had their chairs all the way back. I had closed my eyes. The man slipped his hand under the blanket onto my knee, and then slowly worked up to my thigh. I was wearing jeans and after fifteen minutes or so with his hand between my legs, he unbuttoned them.

"Did you come?" Eduard asked me. "How old were you? How old was he?"

"Oh this was just like, maybe ten years ago," I said. I knew he had pictured me as fifteen or sixteen in the story. "He was about your age, I'd guess. He had a beard and a nice tan. He had wrinkles at the corners of his eyes."

"Did he ask for your number? Did he say anything? He must have known you were awake."

"No, he just pretended like nothing had happened. I watched him get off the plane. I waited for him to look back."

"Why wouldn't he?"

"He didn't," I said. "Of course."

I did not tell him about the time I was in London on my first book tour. I had been drinking and I was unhappy. It was after the dinner and after the event following the dinner, and I had expected the guy I'd talked to all night to try to take me home, and he didn't, and I wanted to say, 'Let's just go back to your place,' because I think he was too shy to ask. So I went to a bar afterward and when some guys started acting weird, aggressive, I walked to a different bar. But I met a man on the street. He was American. He came up to me and said, "I'll give you fifty pounds to suck my cock." He had been drinking too. He was handsome and I went to my knees. He couldn't come, and I started to give up. Then he took me by my hair and one arm and pulled me into an alleyway. He pushed me over a trashcan, pushed up my dress and pulled down my panties.

"I didn't say you could fuck me," I said. "You shouldn't be doing it like this."

He said, "You're right," and raped me in the ass.

There are a lot of stories like that. Once I begin, I want to tell them all. Sitting here in a small, borrowed room in Galveston, I want to forget the whole history of Brett and Eduard and tell each and every one of my other love stories and sex stories and lies. But there are things I can never tell anybody.

THIRTEEN

"I HAVE MOST OF WHAT WE NEED," I SAID. I WAS MAK-
ing dinner for Eduard, who had arrived that morning.
It was a warm day. I had the windows in the kitchen
open and you could smell the flowers from the court-
yard, the wet flagstones and our big cypress trees.

"But what don't you have?" Paul asked. He took a
handful of grapes, and Eduard stood in the doorway
to the kitchen. He wore a T-shirt and a pair of dark
jeans.

"Some onions and carrots, a leek, two bottles of
red wine, and something for everyone to drink. Some

limes for your dad? Gatorade if they have some, and maybe tonic water."

Paul and Eduard went to the grocery store. I hadn't been able to look straight at Eduard yet. If I could drink it would be easier. I broke down and went up to the medicine cabinet for some of Paul's father's Klonopins. I took three, which might have been too many. When Paul came back half an hour later, I was relaxed. He put the bags on the counter and put his arms around me and kissed the nape of my neck. I said, "Where's Eduard?"

"He's in the car," he said. "I remembered egg noodles and thyme."

"Why doesn't he come in?"

"I invited him to the races. Also I think he picked up on your feelings about his visit. He said he would switch to a hotel."

"That's crazy. Should I go out and get him?"

"No, let's just leave him alone." I didn't know whether or not Paul had any suspicions about me and Eduard but I complained about him as often as I could.

"He is high maintenance. No more weeklong visits for Eduard."

"He just got here, for crying out loud."

"You haven't been cooking the past five hours."

"I'm sorry. It's just because he doesn't have kids. He's practically a kid himself. He has to be entertained all the time. Speaking of. I'm late."

"You forgot the wine."

"Shit. I did. Do you need me to go out again and get it?"

"Well, yeah."

"Okay, it's just that we'll be late."

"I don't want to interrupt the boys' games with the ingredients for their dinner. I don't want to have to pack them up and drag them out with me."

He kissed my forehead. "I'll go."

I knew that I could get the wine while his dad watched the kids. Or his dad could get it. Or the kids and I could get it. But for some reason I felt indignant.

I didn't think, Well, after all, I'm making dinner for my lover, who is staying in our home. Or, if I did think that, I thought as quickly, "There is no way for Paul to know that."

I said, "I'm sorry, but I can't make a daube without wine."

Later Eduard often told me: "That day with the wine, when Paul and I had to make two trips. That's when I knew you were in the wrong relationship."

FOURTEEN

"Say what you like about the Mexicans, those Mexicans mothers are doing something right—seems like every Mexican you introduce me to is a doctor, a lawyer, a banker—that doesn't happen on accident. That's a good upbringing. Nurturing."

He looked over his shoulder at Paul's sons, who were eating at the coffee table and watching a show on the computer, and then he gave me a pointed look. Paul's dad had been pouring his own drinks. He took a sip of his Glenlivet and started again.

"These Mexicans have done a lot more good than you might think. Think about their environment. How do you survive in the desert?"

"Camels," Eduard said. He had been drinking too. I did not like his expression.

Paul's father laughed. "Ok, Eduard, your forefathers are in the desert, getting chased by the Spanish, by Christians, Americans, the Texans, so they needed transportable money. Paul, you know this one."

"Diamonds?" Eduard said. "Gold? Mayan gold?"

"Conquistadors, sure. But that was their problem, really, not the solution. Think bigger now. Think the twin towers."

"The twin towers?" I said.

"Surely you don't mean drugs. Drugs and terrorism?" Paul lifted his fork. "Dad—"

"Banking! They're taking over the banks! Right, Eduard? And what's banking? Interest! They're Catholics, sure, but according to the Mexicans making money is a virtue. That's the truth. All through Central America, in fact. That's why the Communists could never get a foothold here, the way they have in South America. It's in their blood. Eduard, back me up here. I heard it from my own banker. He's Honduran and about as good a guy as you ever met. Of course the drug trade has had its impact. Money laundering. That's how the banking originally shifted south. We've got the drug wars to thank for that. Any war you ever heard of, there's a plus side, even for us

44

pacifists. You can't get interest in American banks any more. But the Mexicans figured it all out. Am I right, Eduard? When you think about it, you give a man a dollar and he gives you a dollar and a half back. That's genius. That's pure genius."

I'd had enough. I said, "So how long have you been dating your girlfriend, Eduard? She's a banker too?"

"She's a counselor. A kind of psychiatrist. She works with drug-addicted teens."

"Pure Latin American genius! That's the twin towers connection. Banking in America is dead."

"I guess we've been together six years now?" Eduard looked confused. "We met when one of my partners was having problems with his son. A heroin problem. That's the real drug problem in this part of the world. The kids."

"It's true, that's the unintended consequence," Paul's father said.

"There's no such thing as a free lunch, Eduard."

"I've told you about her," Paul said. He was getting upset. "Her name is Lurisia."

"She's a very beautiful woman," I said. I'd been looking at pictures of Lurisia on Facebook. "She's a swimmer. She's Castilian."

"Have you met her?" Paul asked me. "When did you meet Lurisia?"

Paul's dad gave me a curious, sarcastic look. He thought I was always cheating on Paul.

"She also works in an abortion clinic," Eduard said. "To tell you the truth, I don't approve of that."

"Come on, Eduard," Paul's father said. "You're behind the times. A woman should have as much control over her body as a man. The government doesn't tell you what to do with your cock. They don't tell you to meet with the Feds before you get a vasectomy."

"Dad!" Paul said.

"I don't know," Eduard said. "Perhaps a man should have to meet with a psychologist before a vasectomy."

"You're not thinking it through, Eduard. Suppose you were hooked up to a famous violinist," Paul's dad said. "And they told you you'd be breaking the law unless you stayed in the hospital for nine months."

"Say again?"

"Paul," I said.

"The violinist dies unless your livers are connected. You have to be in bed with the world's best violinist for nine months."

"Man or a woman?" Eduard asked. I left the table and went to play with Paul's sons.

After dessert Eduard came to sit with us and offered to read the boys a book. He had brought books for them and Paul's six-year-old sat in his lap. He read well, and he turned the pages. He offered to read them to sleep. I said, "No, I'll do that."

Paul said, "No, let me."

Putting the kids to bed was something Paul did.

I went to the kitchen to wash the dishes. I heard Paul's dad say behind me, to Eduard, "Those kids just prefer men. You're good with them. I think they scare her. 'Course not everybody's cut out to be a stepmother."

"Can I refill your drink, Don?"

"Why thank you, Eduard. I believe this soldier is dead."

The man has drunk an entire bottle of scotch by himself, I thought.

Eduard came up behind me. He kissed the back of my neck. "Let's go out," he said.

"You're crazy."

"Don't worry. These two are easy. I'll go talk to Paul. You get ready."

FIFTEEN

WE WENT TO THE BAR AT THE RAPHAEL HOTEL ON the plaza. A band was playing. Eduard was drinking whiskey and I had my Coke Light.

He leaned forward to kiss me and squirted whiskey into my mouth. "Let's get a room," Eduard said.

A lawyer type at the end of the bar was trying to catch my eye. Eduard went to the bathroom and the guy with the lawyer-look tried to talk to me, telling me his name. "Are you visiting Mexico City? Do you like the Zócalo?"

When Eduard came back I had brushed him off but he was still looking. Eduard stared him down.

"Do you see that guy?" he asked.

"Yes. He introduced himself to me when you were in the bathroom. He's a real estate developer."

"My father was a real estate developer. I know about real estate developers."

"Hi," Eduard said to the man, who was about fifty and handsome.

His suit was expensive. I looked at his shoes. The same.

He introduced himself to Eduard. They shook hands. Eduard smiled at him warmly. I watched them both look at each other with confidence.

"Ok," Eduard said, and put his arm around my waist. I was still sitting. Eduard told the bartender a room number. He lifted me off the bar stool, and picked up his drink.

"Have a good night," he said to the man, still smiling.

The real estate developer saw how easily and thoroughly he'd been beaten. He smiled thinly back at me and we both understood.

When Eduard got us to the elevator I turned and kissed him with my arms on his back and my hands reaching up for his shoulders. I pressed the whole length of my body against him.

"I liked that," I said, and whispered into his ear. "I'm sopping wet."

We got home just before the sun rose. Paul's dad was on his back in bed next to him, in his clothes, his shoes still on, snoring. His hands were folded behind his head and one elbow was pressed against Paul's ear. I took a shower, made coffee, and fell asleep in a blanket with my head in my arms at the kitchen table.

SIXTEEN

THE FOLLOWING AFTERNOON, EDUARD WAS BESIDE me in my truck, driving. We were coming back to Mexico City after a trip into the country "to look at a new property." We'd brought one of Paul's sons along as cover. He was in the back seat, watching a movie on his iPad.

We wanted to be as close to each other as we could, and it was hard riding next to him and not being allowed to kiss his neck or his cheek or hold his wrist. We had a ten-year-old chaperone.

The rain never stopped. We were halfway back from Calderon, passing cars pulled over on the side of the road. Outside a mile-long maquiladora a jack-knifed semi had flipped over on its side. The driver was standing beside his truck with rain coming down on his shoulders. We'd seen police cars, sand trucks, wet horses and collapsed huts on the wet highway. There was no sun, just low clouds and the rain.

Always, during our time together, it was sun or rain.

"So we're going home?"

"I think we'd better." I glanced with my eyes at the back seat. "I'm ready to go home," Paul's son said.

"It's not even five o'clock. Aren't you hungry, buddy?" Eduard smiled back at him. "This is when civilized people have lunch."

"We can stop and get something to eat if you want," I said.

"I want to go home, Brett. I don't want to eat in a restaurant. I want to see daddy and grandpa. I'm bored."

"Let's drop him off," Eduard said. "I'll run him in and tell Paul that I want you to meet some potential investors. He's got his dad to take care of. I'll tell him you'll sell the idea better than he can. Nobody can sell like a beautiful woman. He knows that."

I gave Eduard a look: he's ten, for Christ's sake, he can understand every word you're saying. People who don't have children don't understand that they are smarter than adults.

"Brett, you can really help me close this deal," he said loudly. "I need your savvy on this one. This will help the hotels. This will really help Paul."

I rolled down the window and let the rain blow into the jeep. "You're getting us all wet!" Eduard said, and he laughed. Then all three of us laughed, we rolled down all our windows, and I was in love again, even more than two minutes before.

SEVENTEEN

When we got to the restaurant Eduard pulled in front and I said, "Can we park here?"

"Let's have a drink," he said. He gave the valet my keys, and told him we'd be back shortly. "Maybe we'll make it back in time to have dinner with them. Maybe we won't."

I knew Paul's dad would be watching our time.

"We really need to be home tonight, Eduard. Paul trusts me. He's not a jealous person. But he isn't dumb."

"I know, I know, I'm sorry," he said. "It's easier for me, because Lurisia stays so busy."

I thought this was a veiled insult to Paul but I didn't say anything.

In the bar a band was playing. Eduard ordered a drink. My phone was buzzing in my purse and I turned it off without looking to see who it was. I was sick to my stomach from the drive and worrying about Paul and his dad. The set ended, and the drummer came to the bar and stood next to Eduard. She ordered a Hendrick's gin and tonic. Slice of cucumber. She was younger than me.

"You guys can play," Eduard said to her.

She was too skinny, and her skin was pocked and covered in heavy makeup. I wasn't concerned.

"Thanks," she said. "We're playing at The Blue Note after this. Eleven o'clock session."

Eduard looked at me. I looked at the drummer. I looked at her with his eyes, and I could see that she wasn't too bad.

"It's a great place," I said.

"Come down. I'll buy you guys a drink. You're a beautiful couple."

"She can't go," Eduard said. "She's too tired. She's going home."

"On a Friday night? Well, that's okay. A woman needs her beauty sleep. You can come alone, if you want. Don't worry, señora, I'll show the proper respect." She patted me on the shoulder, reaching over Eduard.

Eduard told the bartender he would buy her drink.

"No no, thank you very much, but my drinks are on the house. What do you drink?"

"She drinks Coke Light," Eduard said. "I'll have a Jameson's. Not too much ice. You really shouldn't. But thank you."

"A Coke Light," she laughed. "And a Jameson's Irish whiskey for the gentleman please, Bobby. One cube of ice." The drummer told us her name was Maxine, but asked us to call her Max. She gave me a card. Maxine Groove. You can look her up in Mexico City, that's her real stage name.

"That's exactly how I like it," Eduard said about his whiskey. "How did you know?"

All this time I had been filling his glass with ice. Maxine stepped away to go to the bathroom.

"You're seriously going to the Jazz District with that girl?"

"Well, I have the night in Mexico City, I'm not just going to sit in your house."

"I—" There was nothing I could say. "Drink your drink," I said. When Max came back I told her we'd see her down at the club.

"I'm glad to hear you changed your mind," she said. "How's the Coke Light?"

They started to play again. I told Eduard there was a much better club I wanted him to see, where they opened at midnight and played until sunrise.

"Listen," he said. "After my drink we'll get a room. The Four Seasons is five minutes from here. We can order some room service if you're hungry." I was hoping he'd have another drink, get sleepy, and want to go home. This was before I understood he was inexhaustible. He said, "Then we'll go hear some real music. I hate jazz. Did you see that Maxine? What a slut."

I understood that by not going home I was making another small bad real decision, like I had made when I climbed into bed with him that first night.

All these decisions you make for the sake of your lover are little steps you take away from the person you truly love. That's not to say you don't love them both, you do. But one has your heart and the other has your attention.

Then, after many little steps, you turn around and he's so far away that you think, well, he's too far away now. We've gone.

EIGHTEEN

Up in the room, I went into the bathroom to call Paul. When I came out, there was a silver tray on the bed with two hamburgers, french fries, a rose, three whiskies and three Coke Lights. Eduard was sitting on the edge of the bed with his shoes off and his back to me, looking out at the city. I lay down next to him. He didn't move, so I touched his belt loop.

"You got room service."

He took a drink then turned and grabbed my head with both his hands and kissed me, his mouth full of whiskey. I took one of his hands from my head and put it between my legs.

NINETEEN

A LITTLE PAST THREE IN THE MORNING, I WENT TO
the minibar and poured myself a vodka. It was the
first drink I'd taken in two years. I savored it. Then
I had several more. They woke me and my spine
tingled. Dangerously close to sunrise, I woke Eduard, and told him we had to go. Eduard carried me
to the truck. He stumbled and nearly dropped me. "I
can walk!" I said, laughing. We sat in the truck with
the heat blowing and the seat warmers on and kissed.
"Let's go back inside the hotel," he said.

"Eduard. Paul."

He drove carefully, because of the wet streets and the whiskey.

My vodka had had a disappointing effect on me. There was no happy glow like I remembered and expected.

TWENTY

WHEN WE GOT HOME PAUL'S DAD WAS STILL UP, drinking.

"How'd it go with the investors?" He leered at us. "How's the investors? How's the investors, Brett?"

"Go to bed, Don," I said.

"Here, I'll take him," Eduard said.

"I can find my own goddamn bed in this house! This is my son's house! My son!"

I said, "You're going to wake the boys, Don." I was worried about Paul.

"Here, let's have a drink, Don," Eduard said. "Let's have a drink and talk. I think you've got something on your mind." He turned to me. "Why don't you check on the boys, Brett?"

I went to see that Paul was still asleep. Then I made myself a whiskey and went to the guest room to wait for Eduard. I chose whiskey because I wanted Eduard to taste himself on my breath. I knew Paul's dad would end up in our bed again, asleep with his son.

TWENTY-ONE

Eduard woke me up when he came in.

"He's asleep," he said. "Don't worry, they're all asleep."

We made love very gently. I couldn't come, because of all the booze, but I didn't pretend, and he didn't mind.

We lay there and talked. I felt like I could coil up on his belly.

That first drunk when you haven't been drunk in a long time is not really fun. But you recover parts of your personality you'd forgotten, or that had fallen asleep, or were even no longer there.

"You didn't come. Let's make love again."

I don't know why I was suddenly angry with him. But I wanted to hurt him.

"The thing is, you know, Paul, he has. Well, you know what I'm going to say."

He didn't know what I was going to say.

"He has, you know, a big cock. Really big, actually. It's a beautiful cock too. I mean, it's like you think a cock ought to look."

"Like a what's-his-name cock."

"Mapplethorpe."

"Yeah, okay, I got it."

I touched his face and regretted what I'd told him.

"Don't get me wrong, that's not what I'm saying. I love your cock. In fact, his cock just hurts. "

The truth is, I don't know why I said it. Maybe I was trying to be truthful. But he said it didn't bother him. He told me a similar thing happened to him once, when he was with a woman in a movie theater. The movie was about Henry Miller and Anais Nin, and at one point Nin tells Miller, about a rival, "I like your cock better. His is too big."

Eduard told me, "The girl I was with at the movie said, about her husband, 'That's just how I feel. I really like your cock much better than his.'"

"Exactly," I said. "That's how I feel too." I didn't care one way or the other. Though I remembered that when Paul and I first met, I thought his soul-destroying cock meant we were supposed to be together.

Eduard liked to choke me or gag me with his hand while we fucked. He also liked to slap me, hard, in the face and on my breasts, and especially on my legs and ass.

I never told him that I needed him to do these things to me. He intuited it.

"It even scares me," he said, "how violent our sex is." I said, "I don't believe you."

Often while walking to the library, or shopping in Palanco, the women I didn't know pulled me aside on the street to ask: "Is everything alright? Can I help?" I enjoyed that.

TWENTY-TWO

"HEY, I HAVE GOOD NEWS."

"What is it?"

I was excited. I thought Eduard meant good news about us.

"My partners liked Paul's pitch. They're giving him the financing for the property in Costa Rica."

"Oh, okay."

"Don't sound too thrilled."

"I'm glad we got the money. But if Paul's going to Costa Rica all the time, then so are you. And I'm going to be stuck here with the boys. We don't need any more goddamn hotels. We have plenty of money. Tell me you're building a new property in Mexico City and I'll be happy."

"I'll call them back and kill the deal."

"Thank you."

"I'll tell them I can't fuck Paul's wife like she needs it unless we build a resort next to his house."

"Oh you know…" I hung up the phone before I said it. "Fuck you, Eduard."

TWENTY-THREE

HE WAS THE FIRST MAN I EVER MET WHO, WHEN WE were about ten feet away from each another, I could feel a force pulling us together, like there was an electrical circuit that must be completed. When we left each other I could sense its resistance. "Can you feel that?" I'd sometimes ask him, and he'd say, "Of course." Then when it broke there was both loneliness and this elated, dizzy certainty of liberation.

I worried that we brought out the worst in each other.

It's very hard to know, in the early few months of a love affair, what is real and what is imaginary. You find signs and confirmations everywhere. Men passing you on the street stop you to tell you that you're beautiful. Random street signs or airplanes passing overhead prophesize your happiness.

Yet the mind of your lover remains as closed to you as that of a face on a billboard, or a distracted cab driver fiddling with his radio.

Every time I looked at him, when we were happy together, I wanted to put him entirely in my mouth.

TWENTY-FOUR

I'D AGREED TO DO A READING IN MIAMI IN ORDER TO meet Eduard. I was in a Starbuck's in South Beach arguing with Paul on the phone. He was finally having suspicions.

"I can't just get on a plane and come home," I said. "You know I hate Miami. You know how much I hate readings."

"You say you hate readings but then why are you there? Fine. Come home right after. Get a late flight out tonight."

"I'm going out to dinner with my agent tomorrow. It's a big deal, Paul. It's my career. People are forgetting I exist. I'm a writer. I don't manage hotels."

Paul hung up the phone. I tried to call him back three times, but he had taken it off the hook. I called Bella on her cell and asked her if she could get Paul, but she wasn't at the house.

A handsome Swedish man who had been watching me from the corner of the Starbuck's said, "Are you alright?"

"Are you married?"

"No," he said, and smiled.

"Don't," I said. "I've tried it twice now."

TWENTY-FIVE

SADIE HAD INSISTED ON FLYING TO MIAMI TO MEET
me. She had a condo in Coral Gables. I didn't want
her to come. I should never have mentioned it to her.

During an affair you need your closest friends,
because you are falling apart, but then they try to fix
things, which is what you don't want them to do. I
was asking her to help me stop seeing Eduard but I
couldn't stop seeing Eduard.

"Someone's got to keep an eye on you," she said.

"You're one to talk."

"I sleep with guys, I don't fall in love with them."

"Sadie, I'm not joking. I have to meet my agent, and when I'm not with her I'll be with Eduard. You know I'd love to see you. But I don't see how we'll even spend any time together."

"You stood me up when we were in Cancun. We could have had a perfectly good three-way and none of this would have happened. But you had to kick me out of your room and now your whole life is fucked. You're not going to do it this time. You asked me to come."

"Sadie, I didn't invite you to Miami."

"Yes you did."

"What?" I didn't know whether or not I'd invited her. But now I was uninviting her.

"I'm looking up flights right now—if I get on—okay, see you in five hours."

TWENTY-SIX

I MET SADIE AT HER HUSBAND'S CLUB. I TOLD THE
doorman I was meeting Mrs. Brauer. He showed me
to a tall, elegantly dressed cuban man with round
glasses whose job was to stand behind an enormous
desk, who showed me to the maitre d', who gave me
to a waiter, who took me to her table. She was sitting
on a richly upholstered sofa with Swarovski lamps on
both sides and a marble-topped Louis Quinze table
in front of it.

I kept checking my phone for texts from Eduard.
I was trying not to text him.

When I saw Sadie at her table in a cream Van Laack dress, with Celine heels and the open smile of a friend who loves you, I wanted to move to Miami and forget about Eduard, Paul and his children, and my whole life in Mexico City. But I was in love with Eduard, and I loved my husband and his boys, and Sadie ordered Coke Lights for us both.

"Why aren't you drinking wine?" I said. "I'm not in the mood."

Sadie ordered us a charcuterie. I ordered her a glass of white wine.

She said, "Brett. You don't look good."

"Thanks."

"Are you drinking with him?" I lifted a shoulder.

I was about to cry.

She said, "Oof. Are you writing? What's going on with Paul?"

"I'm writing," I lied. Then I said, "I wrote a page. Shit, I don't know." There was a black businessman at the table behind ours. He kept catching my eye and I wondered why. Then I thought, it's because he thinks I'm staring at him.

"I'm not drinking," I said. "It's not like that at all. It has nothing to do with drinking or writing."

Sadie was my friend, but she didn't need to be lecturing me. I said, "Imagine if you had a problem. Some kind of problem. Let's say it was your weight. And sometimes you had a handle on it and sometimes you didn't, and everywhere you went, everyone you met, man, woman and child, counseled you on it. Counseled, advised, or questioned you on it. I always want to tell people: I quit drinking and writing at the same time. Funny coincidence. But I never have to. Before I bring it up they always deny the connection, because everybody knows: I drink, I hurt myself and the people around me, and then I write."

I was shaking. I stood up.

"Honey. Sit down. I'm sorry. It's alright. Does Paul know?" Sadie said.

"About my drinking? Of course not. Sadie. No. God forbid," I sat down. "He'd have already checked me into the hospital."

"No, dummy. About Eduard." I started to laugh. I thought, if I sit here even five minutes longer, I'm going to order myself a drink, whether Sadie wants one or not.

TWENTY-SEVEN

AFTER THE READING, AT THE RECEPTION, EDUARD told me he had brought Lurisia to Miami.

"She insisted at the last minute."

"What? Is she here?" I looked around. It was a charity reading hosted by the Tiffany Circle, and hundreds of people were there.

"No, of course not, I would never do that. She's at the hotel."

"Ok, fine. You're still staying with me. I don't care what you have to do." I would make him pay for this later. "I want to meet her," I said.

"Well, it'd be a little awkward if not."

It was so outrageous that I became very calm. I thought, Okay, Eduard.

I'll stay this calm. I can handle it.

I said, "When?"

"We're all going for drinks with a couple of clients after."

"With clients of yours?"

"So you want it to be just the three of us?" He smiled with one side of his mouth and said, "I'll make it fun. I'll sit by you. I had to put up with Paul for a whole week, Brett."

"You invited yourself!"

I looked around and lowered my voice.

"You're staying with me tonight."

"Fine. I mean, yes. Of course. I don't know how exactly. But yes, it's a deal."

I signed copies of a book I'd written three years before, and Eduard and Sadie chatted. Afterwards we asked her to come with us to meet Lurisia and Eduard's clients. Sadie looked at Eduard and said, with no expression in her voice, "Oh no, I'm exhausted."

The truth is, although I needed her there, I didn't want her to come.

In the taxi, Eduard said he wanted to stop at my hotel before meeting everyone at the bar.

"We don't have time."

"I don't care," he said, and looked at his watch. "Okay, Brett, you're right, we're keeping everyone waiting."

Eduard tried to stop me, but I gave him a blowjob while the driver, a Sikh in a blue turban, kept his eyes on the road.

Eduard's clients were married. One was a prominent architect, and the other was an English indie actress I'd seen in a couple of movies from five or six years ago. They were between my age and his. The woman, who was the more attractive and successful of the two, flirted with Eduard. Lurisia just sat there and took it. I put my foot on Eduard's leg under the table, and the actresses's husband started to flirt with me. No one was flirting with Lurisia and she didn't seem to notice. She was one of those naturally happy people. I don't know whether or not Eduard had told Lurisia we were involved. She looked at me like she knew. I wasn't hiding anything from anyone.

The waiter brought our drinks. He poured my near-beer from high above the glass. I knew how difficult it was to pour a beer like that without foaming it over. I also understood that the waiter was trying to console me for being the only one not drinking. Pouring it like that made it seem like a nice drink.

"That was an elegant pour," I said, and the waiter smiled.

We took two cabs to the party. I made a point of riding with Lurisia. She was an impeccable dresser, with intelligent and sensitive eyes, and we complained about the shopping in Miami. Eduard rode with the actress and the architect.

At the party Eduard took me by the arm and said, "'An elegant pour?' What was that?"

"What are you talking about? The waiter?"

"Yes, Brett."

"He did a nice job of pouring the beer."

"An elegant job. On his pour. My clients thought you were coming on to him."

"I'd say it again. He was pouring it that way deliberately. It's not as easy as it looks."

"People don't say things like that to service people, Brett. It was tacky. My friends thought you were coming on to him."

"You don't know what you're talking about, Eduard." Then I said, "I'm surrounded by savages."

"What?"

"Nothing."

"I heard what you said, Brett."

"You mean, when I called you a savage?"

I was getting very angry.

"Yeah, I'm the savage," he said. "That's priceless."

"A fucking wetback savage."

After I said it I was afraid he'd walk away. But then I saw from his expression that he was afraid I would walk away, and suddenly he didn't look handsome and fearsome. He looked confused, like he didn't know what to do. He looked like a little kid, and I wished I could hold him. He took a sip of his drink, still facing the bookshelves of the apartment we were in, and I fell in love with him again. I reached out and took his fingers in my hand. We made up.

TWENTY-EIGHT

AFTER THE FIGHT, EDUARD SENT LURISIA TO A CLUB with his clients, and spent the night at my hotel. The next morning when I was trying to leave for a meeting with my agent and my editor, he wouldn't stop fucking me. "Stop. I really have to go!" I said, and I couldn't tell how much I meant it. There were often those moments when I meant it but I didn't. That was part of the reason he wouldn't let me out of the room. He wanted me to understand that he mattered more than my meeting did. That I needed him more than I would admit to myself.

I never felt that our sex had anything to do with control, though. It was about need, or about proving ourselves to each other.

Then he started to spank me with the palms of his hands and the backs of his hands. He had a boxer's break on the middle finger of his right hand and I could feel the knuckle every time he slapped me. The more I hurt the harder we fucked. He beat me. I'd had enough and tried to get up. He swore at me and threw me back down on the bed every time I rose. He pinned both my arms behind my back and slapped me with his right hand. Then he slapped my face whichever way I turned it. I cried. "No!" I screamed, and bit him. I drew blood on his shoulder. After the sex was over my ass was bleeding.

He said, "You wouldn't believe what your ass looks like."

"I think I have some idea."

He took a picture with his phone. It was red and purple and there were lines of blood showing through my skin.

I said, "That's my ass."

TWENTY-NINE

THE NEXT NIGHT, I WAS WITH EDUARD AND LURISIA at another party. It was the after party for a wedding. Lines of coke were cut on the tables, and people were drinking guava mojitos. Eduard was embarrassed. He asked me: "Do you mind if I do a line?"

There was a girl who wouldn't leave me alone. She was a writer for Newsweek. She kept telling me how much she'd loved my novel, and she wanted to write a story together on Mexican prisons. She said, "I'm in with the warden in Guadalajara. We could spend the night."

Paul called. He said. "I feel like I'm going crazy." He sounded like he had been crying.

"What do you mean?"

"I mean I'm losing my mind. I never talk to you anymore. You're never home. I don't think you care about me or the boys. When you're not writing you're off at one of the hotels, or talking on the phone. I never see you. I have to go to Costa Rica soon, and I can't count on you to take care of your own family. I feel like you're drinking again."

"Our lives haven't changed," I said. "You know your trip to Guatemala next weekend? Why don't the two of us go? You can leave the boys with your dad. We'll leave on Friday and come back Sunday or Monday. Just us."

Paul said, "You promise?"

I remembered that he was my husband, then, and that I loved him, and that I wanted to go back to him, to go home, to forget all this. You're a wife, Brett, I told myself. You can be a good wife. Paul deserves that. You need it.

I got off the phone and waved to Eduard. He was talking to another woman. A painter. A young girl with a mole on her left cheek, who had done an entire series of canvases with mud.

Eduard put his hand on her wrist and I gave up, came over, and put my arm around him. I didn't know where Lurisia was. He smiled at me.

"Are you ready?" I said. "I think we better go."

"Just a minute." The girl with the mole introduced herself to me. I told her my name and she said, "I know who you are! Of course."

I hate those women who hurt you, and want to be your friend. But often I wish I could do that. Paul's mother was the master. She could say something nice to you that destroyed you for a week.

The bride appeared, back in her wedding dress, but with the bodice pulled down almost to her waist. She'd put her veil back on and she was dancing. Her tits were bouncing all over the place. Her husband said, "Don't come out here like that." She stood up on a coffee table, wobbling.

"I'm married! I'm married! Hey everybody, I am married!" She was waving her ring finger at the crowd. Someone shouted, "You are dancing on the coke!"

The painter said to me, "Pretty."

Eduard said, "Okay, you two."

I gave him a ferocious look. I said to the painter, "You should paint about it. You could do a whole cycle on tits."

The painter said, "You know, that's actually a really good idea.

It's funny you say that. I just sold a painting called 'Tits' in a gallery that represents me in L.A."

At that point I gave up. I said to Eduard, "Come and find me when you're ready to leave."

THIRTY

I WENT TO THE BAR AND ASKED THE BARTENDER TO
pour me a club soda. Then I said, "You know what,
add a couple of fingers of vodka to that. Just float it
on top. There, yes, a little more, thanks."

I drank it standing there and got a second. "Easy
on the soda," I told him.

THIRTY-ONE

SHORTLY BEFORE WE MET, EDUARD HAD BEEN IN LOVE with a singer from Brazil, and I knew he still was. He was in love with both of us, and probably with Lurisia. There were times when I was suffering, thinking about him with Lurisia or the Brazilian or some other woman he might have loved. I thought, I can't lie to him anymore about anything. I'm too tired. I wanted to beg him, can't I just abandon myself to you? Won't you simply take me as I am, exactly as I am, because I am giving myself entirely to you? But then I sensed the need, again, for pretense, if wanted to be attractive to him, if I wanted to be loved in return.

I tried to talk to him about it—and we could talk about those things—and he said he felt the same way. That could not have been a lie.

THIRTY-TWO

After Miami I got Paul out of Mexico City as quickly as I could. We were in bed at the Casas Santa Domingo, just outside Antigua. We'd made love twice that morning, and we were eating warm lobster pupusas in bed. There was coffee spilled on the sheets. Paul had asked for peonies in the room—my wedding bouquet was yellow peonies—and the torn-petaled flowers were everywhere. They'd even put a yellow peony on the silver breakfast tray instead of a rose.

"Do you remember Honduras?" Paul said.

I said, "Do you know the most beautiful thing about this flower?"

"You told me but say it again."

"It has so many petals that it can't open unless ants chew through the casing."

We had a movie on. He had to leave to look at a new property in an hour. "I think Honduras was our best vacation ever," I said.

In Honduras we'd stayed for a week in the tiny Mayan town of Copan, high in the mountains. After a horse ride through the coffee fields we'd bathed in a hot spring—there were a dozen pools—that ran off a mountain stream. The stream itself was boiling: you couldn't touch it. Then a group of middle-aged Japanese women joined us in the deep rock pool. They bathed naked and didn't speak. I had the thought that my dead mother was there, smiling at us, approving. I imagined her thinking: "At last my little lone wolf has figured it out."

The sun set. We had no flashlight and we couldn't find our shoes. I held Paul's hand as we picked our way slowly down the path and across a swinging wooden bridge. Our hotel, a stone cabin that was part of an old plantation built on the ruins of a temple, was lit by dozens of candles. There was no electricity, the mountain air was cold, and there were piles of blankets at the foot of the bed. We only called to speak with Paul's sons and I didn't write or check email. There were no mosquitoes. We had been sober together for a long time and we did not want wine or margaritas. We tanned in the mountains, we were slender. He told me I had never been so beautiful. He had never been so beautiful. I understood, then, that he was the only man I'd ever loved, would ever love.

In the pictures from that time we are sitting so close together, so wrapped up, we could be one person with two heads and four arms and legs, like a Mayan idol.

He said, "Along with our honeymoon, it was our most romantic vacation."

"It feels like a long time ago. I'm tired, Paul."

"Things will get easier soon. I'm opening the new properties. I've been working too much. I love you. Everything's going to be ok. We'll take another vacation soon. The boys are getting older. We could go to Argentina for a week."

"Or Sri Lanka," I said. "Or Madagascar. Get off the continent altogether."

We made love again.

When Paul got dressed and left to drive to the coast, I called Eduard. "I miss you," I said. "What are you doing?"

"I miss you so much I feel sick. I can actually feel it."

I was glad. "I know. It's like someone's pulling on a wire that's tied up inside your chest. It hurts. I can talk for almost an hour. How long can you talk?"

The phone beeped. It was Paul. I ignored it.

"I can talk," he said. "Are you guys having fun? How's the hotel? I've always wanted to stay at that place."

"I wish you were here. Paul's happy."

"That's good. He deserves it."

"I deserve to be fucking you. And I don't want to have to wait another week before we are."

When Paul came back from his meeting I was asleep. He got in bed beside me and told me about his ideas for the new hotel. He was excited about the bathtubs. "They'll be carved out of quartz. I didn't even know that was possible. You'll be in the bath, outside, watching the sea. I'm so grateful we got away. Let's go to dinner. I'm going to keep my tie on. I want to be dressed up."

He was so happy. I was miserable, and on the way back from the bathroom I ran to the room and drank two bottles of vodka from the minibar.

I kept having visions of Eduard, and I couldn't sleep. I was losing weight.

THIRTY-THREE

I WAS BACK IN MEXICO CITY AT THE UNIVERSITY library working on my new novel. Sitting at the computer, I could feel that I hadn't been writing in a long time. But I had energy from being sad and being angry. It was coming back fast.

"That's your phone ringing," the librarian said. "Señora? Señora Ramsey? That's your phone."

I jumped up, answered the call and headed for the stacks to talk, thinking it was Eduard.

It was Paul. He was talking very quickly. He said, "Have you been talking to Eduard? About a new contract? Has Eduard been calling you about business? Is there some deal we're doing with Eduard that I don't know about? Is there a problem?" He was reaching for any possibility. "Your cellphone bill is almost six hundred dollars. It's all calls to Eduard's number."

"I'm coming home." I hung up.

When I got there he was at the gate, smoking. He had the phone bill in his hands. It was the first time I had seen him smoking since he quit four years before, when the doctor told him that the boys' allergies might be caused by secondhand smoke.

I got out of the car. He threw the phone bill at me. The pages flew up, fell down.

"Get the fuck out of here."

"Paul."

"I'm taking the boys to San Salvador while you move out. Then I'm going to divorce you. Then I'm going to kill that greasy motherfucker. Then I'll put him out of business. Then I'll destroy his reputation. He's not the only one with friends in this country. I know what kind of deals he's doing. 'Banking.' Banking my ass. He's a money launderer. He's a fucking vacuum cleaner."

"Paul."

"Do you realize he's borrowed on every one of his properties from half a dozen different banks? That's illegal, Brett. It's called pyramid financing. Do you even know where his money comes from?"

"I love you, Paul."

"He's a fucking drug dealer. He's a glorified drug dealer. He cleans drug money for a living."

"Paul, it's not what you think. I don't care about him. It's over. It means nothing."

"Do you know how many women he fucks? Do you know how many women he's fucked in the past month? Do you know how many times he's tried to get me to go to a whorehouse?"

The fight continued inside. I was glad he let me in. The boys hid from us. It went on for more than two hours the same way. Paul planned to leave in the morning, but he agreed to let me spend the night. I went to sleep on the far side of my side of the bed, but I reached out with a foot to touch his leg. He let it rest there. I thought, This is a hopeful sign.

I woke to shouting. "Look at this, you slut!"

"What?" The room was dark and I was still asleep.

"You whore!" He threw my cellphone, and it shattered on the wall. I climbed out of bed to get it but he beat me there.

"Just look."

"Okay," I reached out for the phone and he jerked it back. I said, "What does it say?"

"Look at it! Don't try to take it!" He held it in his hand and showed me the screen.

There were four texts. They were between Paul and Eduard, who was listed in my phone as "Supermart Pharmacy."

Paul (to Supermart Pharmacy): What r u doin?

Supermart Pharmacy: Nothing. What are you doing?

Paul: Fighting with Paul.

Supermart Pharmacy: Oh, I'm sorry. Be kind to him.

I tried to take the phone from Paul. I wanted to text Eduard and tell him that he had been texting with Paul, not me. Paul went to the bathroom and dropped my phone into the toilet. He said, "Get out."

At three a.m. I checked into The Raphael. The desk clerk was carefully groomed, and she gave me and my torn jeans and thousand-dollar heels a look of sympathy and superiority. The hotel room was white, silent and uncluttered. It was a nice hotel room. I thought about the hotel room I'd stayed in the night I left my first husband, years before, in Dallas. I went to the bathroom and saw I'd left our house so quickly I hadn't rubbed my face cream in all the way. I had a very tiny smear above my cheekbone. I thought, Well, ready for round two.

PART TWO

ONE

"I WANT YOU TO TRY ON ENGAGEMENT RINGS," EDUARD said. "Just for fun."

We were in San Salvador. He'd found us a hotel with a beach we could walk on. We woke early and walked along the beach for more than an hour. We climbed a hill covered with vines and on the other side there was a sea cave. We took off our shoes and our clothes and put them on a high rock and swam naked. We were in the water for half an hour and Eduard said, "Look!" and caught his own wallet floating in the water. He found my shoes in the surf. There was no beach left by our cave and we had to swim out beyond and around the rocks with our clothes in our hands to get back to land. I had wanted to make love on the sand in that cave.

I was hungry but I was hungry in that nice beach way, when you don't have to eat if you don't want to.

He rented a convertible. We'd never driven together in a convertible before and I turned the radio up loud. It was not hot in El Salvador that May. He told me that we should put the top up when we were on the highway but I didn't want to put it up. We never put the top up on that car once the whole week we were in San Salvador. It never rained.

"Well, this is the place," he said. It was a narrow street but the sun came straight down into it. A dog walked up to our car and started to sniff it. The car was expensive enough that no one would mess with it, for fear of who might own it.

Everywhere you went in Central America, at this time, if you were in a town or a city, you saw serious young brown skinny men with large rifles and sub-machine guns. I expect it is still the same way today. Two of them stood on each corner of this street. One smoked a cigarette and watched us shyly.

We went into the jewelry store. It was hidden in a bank building, upstairs, and we walked through several anonymous offices and two locked doors before sitting down in a small wallpapered room. They brought us glasses of champagne. I drank mine without hesitating and asked for another. Eduard frowned.

We all sat at a small, elegant table. I'd taken off my wedding ring. "She likes emerald cuts and cushion cuts," Eduard explained to the jeweler. He was a chubby man with slicked-back gray hair in a black suit. He lay a diamond cloth open on the table.

"One carat? A carat and a half?" He had an Italian accent.

"Nothing under two," Eduard said. "She likes fancy colors, if you have a vivid yellow. She also likes pinks."

"We don't have any pink diamonds over half a carat, Señor Carranza."

My best friend from college wore a two-carat pink diamond for her wedding ring. She was an attorney in Mexico City, and she handled some business for us. Eduard had met her and he knew I admired her ring.

"I do have a lovely three-stone ring with quarter-carat pinks on either side. The center stone in a carat-and-a-half round, D Flawless. But of course I can call in a larger stone for you. I have the papers on several pinks from our partner store in Rio de Janeiro."

I had a third glass of champagne. Eduard had a second. He looked at a dozen loose diamonds and chose a 2.45 carat cushion cut, F VVS1, $88,500. The jeweler placed it on my the back of my closed fingers and said, "Wear it out into the sunlight." The security guard started to walk out with us but the salesman brushed him back into the store.

We stood in the sunlight and looked at the diamond. I said, "It's not what I had in mind."

"It's beautiful," Eduard said. He put his hand on my back.

"I'm not sure."

We were playing.

The salesman said, "She wants a pink. She's right." He gave Eduard his card.

"If I can call you, sir, I'll arrange several pinks to show you and the lady." He bent toward me with a smile. "I can have them here by Wednesday."

"I'll call you," Eduard said. He took the stone off my fingers, looked at me for a moment, and returned it to the man, who took it from him with the diamond cloth and cleaned it before tucking it in his breast pocket. He went back inside after shaking hands. Eduard put his arm around my waist. "Thank you," he said. "That was fun."

TWO

WE WENT TO A LOCAL PLACE HE KNEW NEAR THE cathedral and got drunk on the owner's private collection of Peruvian brandy. I decided to drink as much as I wanted. I wanted to celebrate.

I looked at Eduard. I said, "I'm free. You don't know how good it feels."

"Are you hungry?" Eduard said.

"No. Are you?"

"I'll order a few things. The food's good here."

When I went to the bathroom I looked in the mirror. My face looked strange. Careful, Brett, I thought.

I splashed my face with water, and I went back to the table. I noticed the waiter seemed nervous. I ordered another round, and I thought, That waiter's afraid of me.

"That jeweler liked your chain," I said to Eduard. I had given him a heavy 18kt gold Bulgari chain when we were in Miami. It was the only piece of jewelry I'd ever given a man.

"He was too busy checking out your cleavage," he said.

I took a big swallow of my drink. It was already empty. I took a sip of Eduard's and waved to the waiter. "Do you take that necklace off?"

"I never take it off. You know that."

"I mean, when you're fucking Lurisia."

He frowned.

"Does it slap her tits?"

"What?"

"You heard me. Does your necklace slap Lurisia's tits, when you fuck her? Or anybody. When you fuck your whores."

I finished his brandy. The waiter came to the table and I ordered two more.

"Can you make a pisco sour?" I asked him. "Two pisco sours."

"Just one, for the lady," Eduard said. "Brett, what's up? A minute ago we were having a perfectly pleasant conversation. I think you should eat."

"Do they grab it. Your whores. When you eat them out."

"For Chrissake, Brett."

"I just want to hear about your necklace, Eduard. The one I gave you. Do they wrap it around your cock?"

He stood up from the table. "Brett, I don't know what's come over you. But the way you're talking to me is not—"

"Is not what? Now that I'm finally telling the truth. Is not what, Eduard? Tell me. Tell me the truth for once."

"Come with me, Brett. Let's get something to eat in the room."

"I'm staying right where I am. You go, then. Get out of here."

"I'm going back to the hotel."

"I guess it just lays between their tits," I said. "The chain I mean. Unless you're about to come. Then it probably slaps them." The waiter brought me a pisco sour. I said, "You switch it around backwards, between your shoulder blades, the same way you do when you fuck me."

"Goodnight, Brett."

"I'll let you know when I make up my mind. Go to sleep. If I want to I'll wake you up."

"We can talk in the morning."

THREE

It was the first time Eduard had seen me in a blackout. He told me about it the next day. I didn't quite believe him. I told him I was sorry. But still it was strange because it seemed to me like we'd only been at the bar for half an hour.

"Listen, I know you don't want to hear this right now, but I have to have a drink."

"Let's have mimosas. Room service."

FOUR

PAUL HAD STAYED WITH HIS PARENTS FOR TWO WEEKS
and now he and his sons were back in the house. I
had promised Paul that I would be moved out, but
I had not packed any more than the first suitcase.
I hadn't even gone home. I had been living at The
Raphael and going on vacation with Eduard. I had
been shopping. I drank when I shopped. I had begun
to dress differently, in expensive clothes. I was popu-
lar with the salespeople. I wrote a story about a man
who kills a Mexican prostitute. Then I wrote one
about an effeminate old man who falls in love with

a twenty-year-old. I sent them to my agent and she placed them immediately. She wrote, "Whatever it is you're doing, don't stop."

I had also promised Paul that I wouldn't see Eduard. Eduard had told Paul that his relationship with me had been a fling and Paul believed him, though he insisted that one of Eduard's partners take over our business banking. I knew the most important thing I could do was stay in touch with Paul, but I couldn't make myself call him. I didn't want to lie to him.

But Eduard was always trying to make me call him. "If he doesn't hear from you, he'll think we're together," he said. "How hard is it to lie, Brett? How many lies have you told Paul in your life? How many has he told you?"

"He doesn't really lie."

"You think he tells you the truth about everything?"

"This is different. I can't lie to him. I can't just say you're not here. Just lie about everything that's going on. I'm not like you, Eduard. You're like a master thief who sees a kid stealing candy and says, 'See, everybody lies.' Most people don't really lie that much. It doesn't come naturally."

Eduard could lie to Lurisia—they still lived together—to his clients, his boss, to me, to friends, all of them, effortlessly. I'd seen him do it. He said that like most highly intelligent people, he was a liar.

"I'd rather tell him the truth. I'd rather everybody just know the truth," I said, "Why do you care what I do, or who I tell? You don't tell anyone. You hide me like a secret. You're ashamed of me."

"What possible difference could it make to Paul whether what you're telling him is true of false? One difference. Whether or not you're hurting him. Hurting him and us."

I wanted Eduard to be proud of me. I wanted him to reveal the truth about us. I wanted Eduard to tell Lurisia, his parents and his friends: I'm in love with Brett. But you can't make your lover do that. Once I worked at a magazine and the publisher sent around a folded memo that read: "I demand respect!" Same situation here. You can't make your lover love you. At least not by direct means.

"Fine. You win. I'll call him."

Bella answered. Bella hated me now. "That Brett," she said, "is on the phone." She gave the phone to Paul, and I lied to him for twenty minutes. I told him I wasn't moved out yet, I had been with my mother—she was sick. I could hear him hearing the lies. He understood: I was in love with a Mexican banker.

FIVE

On a flight back to Mexico City from visiting
Eduard in Panama I upgraded myself to first class
at check-in. Waiting for the plane, I had three double margaritas. They seemed like light pours to me,
but when I sat down I remember feeling a bit odd.
A middle-aged woman sitting across the aisle from
me frowned when I ordered a drink before the plane
took off. She was probably about my age but she was
dressed in St. John. The flight attendant brought me
a bottle of red wine and I held it in my lap.

I tried to be friendly with the woman across the aisle, but I could hear myself slurring my words. I was probably repeating myself. The next thing I remember distinctly was when she said, "Would you please watch your language."

She took an embroidering kit out of her bag and started to needlepoint. "I like the pattern," I said.

She ignored me.

"Have you been sewing for long? That's quite a hobby." I poured myself a glass of wine and drank it. The bottle was full so the flight attendant must have brought me another.

"Is that for your mom? Or for a friend?" She kept on sewing.

"My maid sews. I mean, that's not an insult. My grandmother sewed. She did embroidery."

The woman ignored me.

"It used to be a sign of effluence. Aff—affluence. It is still, having the leisure to needlepoint."

The woman put her work down and turned to face me. She said very distinctly, "Can you stop talking?"

I reached up an arm and pushed the flight attendant call button. When the flight attendant came, I said, "This woman beside me just threatened to stab me with that needle."

"I'm sorry, ma'am?"

"The woman tried to stab me. Said she was going to take the plane down."

The needlepoint woman protested.

"Ma'am, is there a problem here?"

"She pointed her needle at me. She said she was going to jab me. The needle needs to go. Or she needs to go in back. I mean, one or the other. You pick. She's crazy."

"I don't know what she's talking about." The woman seemed nervous.

"You know, you know. You can't fool these people. They're experts."

"Ma'am, I think you should calm down."

"I am not safe in this seat. I think she should put that needle away or be taken off the plane. I mean, if you need to land this thing, I understand." I gave the woman with the needle a look like, See what you just did? No more first class for you, lady.

The flight attendant was looking at my wine. She left. Then a man in a blue shirt and khakis appeared.

"Ma'am, I'm the air marshal on this flight."

"Finally."

"Ma'am, I'll need you to come with me."

I didn't know where to put my wine bottle. The latch on the seat-tray beside me wasn't working. Then my tray wouldn't latch up.

"I'll handle that for you, ma'am," the marshal said, and took my bottle of wine.

I followed him up to the galley.

"Ma'am, I want you to understand this is serious."

"I unnerstand."

"The accusations you have made are serious. You do understand that."

"Yes, sir."

"Tell me again. What happened?"

"Yes, officer."

"Tell me."

"Yes, sir."

"Ma'am, you're not answering my question. I'm asking you to tell me what happened between you and the other passenger."

"The needle. She's got a needle."

"Okay."

"She said she was going to take the plane down."

"You're positive? You don't think you might have misunderstood her, or ... anything like that?"

"No, sir."

"The passenger next to you in seat 3C told you that she was going to take the plane down with her sewing needle. That's what happened?"

"As far as I can tell."

"Ok ma'am. This is what happens next. So that you are very clear. We are going to have to land the plane. I am going to have to call the Mexican police. They will take each of you to interrogation rooms, and you will both be questioned."

"Do you think she may have been kidding?"

"Well, I wasn't there. I am asking you."

"She looks harmless. She looks like my grandmother."

"Well ma'am, the charges you made are serious, but I can see you've been drinking, and so I'm just going to put you in the back of the plane. But I want you to know this is not a game. You're on an international flight."

"I'm sorry if I caused any confusion. You know, she's just sewing. My grandmother does it too. She's just sewing. A person should be allowed to sew. On a plane."

"Let's get you back to your seat."

"You can't sew without a needle. She's just. You know. Needlepoint."

"Yes ma'am."

They moved me out of first class, to the back of the plane. I didn't protest. I tried to order a whiskey but the flight attendant in economy told me they were out of whiskey. "A vodka? A beer?" He ignored me.

SIX

WHEN WE LANDED I WAS ALMOST SOBER. I CALLED Eduard from the taxi to The Raphael. "I almost got myself arrested."

I told the story, and I was surprised that Eduard laughed the whole way through.

"You got what was coming to you. She won. She had old lady magic. Besides, it sounds like you were hammered."

He was in his and Lurisia's apartment. I was getting nearer asking him when he planned to move out. One of you has to move out first, I reminded myself.

I was the one to move out first when I left my first husband, too.

"What's old lady magic?" I said.

"How they cut in lines, all that."

"She wasn't even old! She was my age. And I wasn't that drunk. I wasn't even drunk enough for anyone to notice."

"Obviously not," Eduard said. But he was laughing with me, and it was nice, to laugh with someone about one of my drunk stories. I'd missed that when I was sober.

SEVEN

A MONTH, PERHAPS TWO MONTHS WENT BY. I STARTED asking to come back home. Paul's family wanted a divorce, the quicker the better. His therapist said that he deserved better.

"People have affairs, Paul. It doesn't mean the marriage ends. It means we have problems. I'm sorry. I did a horrible thing. But I love you. I love our sons. I want to come home."

"It's too much. I can't do it any more."

"The first time we are really on the rocks you just divorce me?"

"It's not the first time, Brett. I put up with your drinking for six years. You tried to kill yourself with my son five feet away from you." He had never called him, "my son." He made a point of saying, "our sons," and even, "your sons." The suicide attempt was from my novel.

It had happened, but not the way I told it in the book. He was quoting my own fiction back at me.

"You know as well as I do that suicide attempt was ridiculous. I was hanging myself with a sheet, Paul. Our son was asleep. I was trying to get your attention. I was trying to tell you that I'd been secret drinking for three years without having to face the consequences."

"That's my point. Three years of lying. Not to mention all the other lies. It's not worth it. I can never trust you again. You're a sociopath." When in years past friends of ours had joked with him about my lies and exaggerations, Paul had always said, "Brett is the most honest person I've ever met." He wasn't joking. He thought I didn't tell the fake social lies that everybody else did. He knew I never pretended to be someone other than who I was. He also genuinely believed that he was the one person I would never lie to.

EIGHT

PAUL AND I MET IN A FILM CLASS ON ALMODOVAR AT the University of Texas at Austin shortly after I left my first husband. During seminar breaks I pretended to smoke so that there was a reason to hang out with him. After seminar one afternoon we went with a friend of his to have beers and play pool at The Showdown on Guadalupe. It's a bar that people who know Austin know about. He was skinny, his blonde hair brushed his shoulders then. He had small wrists and narrow shoulders, and I liked the way he dressed. He wore these worn out tweed coats—all wrong for the weather, but right on him, and he had a clumsy way of bending over the pool table that I liked. He liked to drink. Everyone who met him immediately told him, if the opportunity presented itself, that he had astonishing eyes. They are enormous, and a color of blue I have not seen anywhere else. Unlike most everyone's eyes, they are almost always the same color.

NINE

HE WAS IN THE FILM STUDIES GRAD STUDENT STUDY lounge on the third floor of Ryan Hall in a collared windowpane shirt, green crewneck sweater and grey wool slacks. He sat on the sofa with his legs crossed, like a girl, I thought. Later he told me that actually it is a woman who should cross her legs at the ankle, and a man at the knee. He was talking to one of the famous visiting professors. I came into the office and sat down on the other side of the sofa.

"I'm hungry," I said. "Are you hungry? Do you want to get some lunch?"

TEN

WE SAT OUTSIDE AT THE SHADY GROVE. WE BOTH had Bloody Marys. I think we had four each. I had a plate of vegetables with a smoked green chili sauce—I was a vegetarian at this time, and had dropped to one hundred and five pounds—and he had a fried chicken sandwich with gravy, which is the best thing there. I had to drive drunk to my seminar.

In the next few days I disentangled myself from relationships with three other men I was dating at this time. After one date with Paul I knew I didn't want to see other men. Then he asked me out.

When he picked me up for dinner I was in a short, green dress. I was wearing too much eye make-up. I noticed he had bought new pants and a new jacket for the date. He didn't know that was one of my favorite things about him—nothing he wore was new.

At the restaurant, walking in, I called him "Sam." Sam was a man I had been dating. Paul missed a step and then continued walking as though he hadn't noticed. Inside I apologized, and explained that I wasn't seeing Sam anymore.

After we opened our menus and he chose a bottle of wine I said, "Let's eat a lot of food."

For years afterward he repeated that remark back to me, as the first time he knew that he might fall in love with me.

After dinner, Paul came back to my apartment and we sat on the sofa together. It was an enormous sofa. It came with the apartment and looked like it had been made in the late seventies with burlap bags. I'd bought two blankets at Urban Outfitters to try to make it presentable but it didn't quite work.

I was apologizing for the sofa. I was apologizing for the whole apartment. "Would it be alright if kissed you?" he asked. We kissed on the sofa and he kissed like a hungry tiger might make out with you.

"Hey, slow down," I said after a minute. "There's no rush."

"Are you making fun of the way I kiss?"

"No. You're a great kisser. I just—there's no hurry. We can kiss all night."

He changed his kiss then and we kissed more gently, calmly, and deeply. I was reassured because I saw we would be able to kiss together after all.

If you can't kiss each other, there's no point in continuing.

Eventually we moved to the bed, and he had my hand between my legs, and then his face between my legs, but I wouldn't let him take down my leggings. I was squirming.

"This is ridiculous," he said at last. "You're obviously as frustrated as I am. Let's have sex."

"No," I said, and pushed him away. "We can kiss if you want. But we're not having sex. I don't know you well enough yet."

"You know me. Don't lie. Look at me." He kissed me again, and we kept our eyes open. I squeezed his hips between my legs. "Tell me you don't want me to fuck you."

"No!" I said. I laughed and wriggled away. We wrestled.

"Okay, okay," he said. "Let's have a glass of wine."

Months later, Paul asked me, "Why didn't you sleep with me that night?"

ELEVEN

CHEATING ON YOUR HUSBAND IS A LOT LIKE DOING cocaine. It's rarely pleasurable, but try quitting.

Eduard left Lurisia and moved into a new place. At night in his condo we often sat on his balcony and listened to Bob Dylan and watched the people in the streets below. We'd take pillows from the bed, I'd be between his legs with his arms around me and I'd turn my head so that we could kiss.

"Next summer we'll get some of those misting things for out here," I said. "That way we can come out all summer long. We could sleep out here. With a big mosquito net."

"Good idea," he said, and the way he said it, like we would never make it to next summer, made us both quiet for a few minutes.

"Does Paul want you back?" he asked.

"That's the worst part," I lied. "He wants it so much. But I can't go back. I'm in love with you. A week would go by and I would be on a plane to you again."

That part was true.

TWELVE

I DIDN'T DRINK WHEN I WAS ALONE IN MEXICO CITY, mostly, but I was always drinking when I was with Eduard. I always drank on the way to see him, and sometimes on the way back.

He didn't like to drink with me, now, so I'd drink when he wasn't around.

One night, coming back from a trip Eduard and I took to Peru, I had a black out. I remember buying margaritas for everyone at the airport bar. Eduard and I had taken separate flights home. I was on a layover and I didn't know what airport I was in. I woke up in the hospital in Mexico City. I had cracked my head on the stone stairs outside the hotel. Eduard said I had called him late that night. "You said you'd been arrested, and then they let you go."

The next day, Paul came to get me at the hospital.

"You're not stable. You have to get sober, Brett. You can't live in a hotel."

I was picking at the staples in my hair with my fingers.

"I want to spend time with the boys," I said. "I miss them so much. You don't know how much I love them. Even if you're not going to talk to me, I have to see the boys."

He had been dating friends of ours in Mexico City—he'd even been sleeping around—but I knew he hadn't fallen in love. His parents were spending a lot of time in town. Sadie kept trying to talk me into moving in with her in Galveston.

"The boys miss you," Paul said. "How about we make a deal. You go back to Minnesota and dry out. You loved it there. Go to Hazelden and I'll think about things."

"I was miserable."

"It worked, Brett. If you'll spend thirty days there, you can see the boys once a week. Or every other weekend, even, if you get an apartment. They can't spend the night with you at a hotel."

THIRTEEN

I'D GO SEVEN DAYS, TEN DAYS, TWO DAYS SOBER. THEN
in Puerto Vallarta or some other city I'd take a drink.
By this time, I hid it from everybody—even Eduard
thought I'd quit.

I was back to my old tricks.

When a normal person walks into a restaurant she
looks for the best table, the most cheerful location,
a sunny spot or an intimate corner. Or she doesn't
think much about it at all: she lets the hostess or her
date decide. A secret drinker maps the restaurant like
a bank robber maps a score. She locates the bar, the

women's room, and the (usually, small) group of tables that allow her to pass the bar while on her way to the bathroom without her date being able to see her. Supporting pillars are good; ideally, she wants a blind spot where he cannot spot her even if he turns his head. A man will watch his woman as she comes and goes in a way that a woman will not watch her man, not because he is suspicious of her, but because he likes to watch her move. The secret drinker looks for restaurants with bars next door: if necessary, she can exit out the back, take a quick drink at the neighboring place, and come back again. On his first drink the secret drinker will tip the bartender at least as much as the cost of the drink, so she's made a friend. The secret drinker will wait outside the bathroom, motion to her waiter, ask him to bring a drink—"a double vodka, I'll just drink it right here, and pay for it now"—if there is no way to approach the bar, or no bar in the restaurant. She will casually flirt with the bartender or the waiter to try to make him part of the game. The secret drinker can open a bottle of beer with any hard object: the edge of the lock in the bathroom stall, a counter top, the nut on a pipe, a key in her pocket, in desperation, her thumbnail. The secret drinker always carries cash with her. She cleans out half the bottles in the minibar and refills them with water while her lover is shaving. She is quick to pour her lover a drink if he wants one—though the bottles she's drunk will be in the back of the refrigerator, where he is unlikely to take one. Above all, the secret drinker keeps her lover drunk. Because a sober lover can tell if you've been drinking. He keeps track of time and how often you've been to the bathroom. He notices you've been gone to the convenience store for half an hour when it should have taken ten minutes. With a drunk lover you can drink all night long.

FOURTEEN

At times when I was very drunk Eduard would record what I had said the night before. "No post mortems" had been a rule, but we were past that. It started when he went to the bathroom and saw I had peed on the floor. He mentioned it to me when he got back into bed—he woke me up to tell me. And he turned on his phone so that I would have to hear it.

"I doan see what the big deal is."

"Brett. You were too drunk to find the toilet."

"Did you fuck me while I was passed out?"

"Let's go back to sleep."

"Did we have sex? Is your come inside me?"

"Brett. Can you hear yourself."

"How many times did you fuck me when I was out?"

"I can't believe the things you're saying."

"For me, Eduard, sex and emotion are all bound up together. Most of the—95 percent of the sexual experience I had, was when I was—you know what? You were right before, we're not right for each other. I'm not right for you."

Silence.

"It's fine. Really, it's all fine. It's lucky we found out when we did. I'm just glad we're finally telling the truth."

"Brett, go to sleep. Everything is alright."

"Yup. You did. It's for the best. I'm just glad we finally got it out into the open."

"Brett, I never said that."

"You don't love me. You just took the first woman who came along. You bastard."

"Shh."

"No matter how hard I try, it's never good enough for you. Nobody can say—nobody can say I didn't try."

"Brett."

"Don't say, 'Brett.' You're ashamed of me. When I'm the one who should be ashamed."

"I'm going. I'm going to get a different room in the hotel."

"Everyone knows about your sluts. Your whores. Paul told me. He's told everyone. It's like a joke. All your friends know. A man can be a slut too. Look at yourself in the mirror."

Insights of this kind by the blacked-out me.

FIFTEEN

I TOLD HIM I HAD A SECRET FORTUNE THAT I WOULD be awarded by my dead grandparents when I turned forty. "Hundreds of millions, neither one of us will ever work again." I told him about imaginary stories and novels I had written or published. I told him about famous men in pursuit of me, men I spurned for his sake. I promised suicide.

It is hard, even for a practiced drunk, to take responsibility for things she says or does during a blackout. When you have no recollection of doing something, it's as though it's been done by an evil stranger who hates you, and who has decided to possess your body in order to destroy everything that you love. As a way of murdering you.

"You're like Dr. Jekyll and Mr. Hyde," Eduard said.

"I've never heard that one before."

"This isn't a joke. Why won't you just admit it when you're drunk? You need professional help, Brett."

"I'm not drunk half as often as you think I am."

"If that's true, you're in even worse shape than I thought. Alcoholism I can understand. This other person you become, when you're in one of your fugues"—that's what he called my drunk moods, when I was at my worst—"is dangerous. You don't know what you're doing. You could get hurt, Brett. You could be raped. There's no telling what could happen."

"My psychiatrist says I'm fine as long as I stay sober. And I'm telling you, I've quit drinking. Give me a chance. Let's go to Cancun, where we first met. We'll spend a few days there and then drive down the coast. I'll show you. Anyway, I want to see that new place in Valladolid. Those people are making a name for themselves."

"What place? I don't know about it."

"Some couple Paul told me about. He says they're knocking him off. It will be fun to look. We'll be like spies."

I don't know what might have happened next if Eduard hadn't agreed.

SIXTEEN

IN CANCUN I KNEW I WAS GOING TO STAY SOBER.
Since Paul had tossed me out I realized how much I
needed to see my boys. I wanted Eduard to believe in
us. I didn't want to wake up to the forensics of ghastly
fights I didn't even remember.

His flight came in to Mexico City and I bought
him a whiskey at the bar.

"I don't have to drink," he said. "Honestly, I don't
want to."

"It won't work that way," I said. "I have to be
sober for myself. And if you stop drinking just for

me you'll resent me. Or you'll only drink when we're not together and you'll want a drink when we are. Or you'll have more fun when you're drinking with your friends and I'll seem dull because you never get to have a drink." This last certainty was the one I feared the most.

"I don't think any of those statements are correct. I'm happy to stop drinking. It's not that big of a deal for me."

"It isn't now," I said. "But that's because you're free to drink. If you feel like you can't, it's going to come between us. Just trust me on this one."

"Did it come between you and Paul?"

He had me there. Once I was properly sober, the time Paul and I had together when we weren't drinking was perhaps the best time of our marriage.

"Am I with Paul now? And what's the first thing he did when we split up? Started drinking again."

It was true. Paul was drinking with his dad. I spent hours lying in bed in my hotel room, imagining the things they were saying about me. Or that, worst still, they were drunk together and I never came up.

"Fine, fine, I'll drink the whiskey. Hell, I could use it. You look great. I've got to go to the bathroom, I'll be right back."

I knew he was lying about how I looked. And I knew he was texting Lurisia in the men's room.

SEVENTEEN

The hotel in Cancun was new and extravagant, but too big. Eduard knew the owner and I was relieved when he told me that we didn't have to go out with him. We were on the beach. The room was made of blue marble—Italian rather than Mexican—pale yellow silk, and glass.

"Let's change hotels," I said.

"This is the best hotel in Cancun. They just built the damn thing. It's gorgeous."

"It's great," I said. "Thank you. But I don't feel like we're safe here. Do you know what I mean? Let's find a little place. I don't even care if we're on the beach. I want to feel like I have you all to myself."

"You're crazy," he said. "Whatever Brett wants, Brett gets." He made love to me on the bed, and then he got on the phone while I took a bath and found us a different place.

EIGHTEEN

IT WAS ONE OF THOSE VACATION PLACES WHERE NO one minds if a couple is falling all over each other. Our new hotel room had windows on three walls. One was above the bed, and another overlooked a stairwell. Through both windows we could see palm fronds and bougainvillea in pink, red and orange, and many other tropical flowers I didn't know. We could hear the birds screaming in the trees and smell the sea. I hadn't been drinking for almost a week now and my sex drive was back. I insisted that we keep the windows open and the curtains back when we had sex. We were noisy in bed.

"At least let me shut them," he said. "If I can't pull the curtains."

Eduard had my arms behind my back, my legs between his, and he was fucking me as hard as he could from behind while I groaned. I saw a man who looked Cuban position himself behind a post on the stairs. He was five feet from our bed. He peered around the post every few seconds and caught my eye. He smiled at me.

"I can never predict what you're going to be prudish about," I said, after we finished.

"I'm Catholic. I'm shy," he said, smiling. "Plus, I mean this is not exactly prudish. We are being exhibitionists."

"I don't see what there is to be ashamed of."

But I couldn't hide my expression and he knew I enjoyed it.

NINETEEN

OUR HOTEL DIDN'T HAVE A POOL, AND LATER WE WENT
to the pool at a property Madonna owned or had
owned and I ordered Eduard a drink so that we had
a right to swim. A couple who had rented a cabana
told us we could lay in their deck chairs. I was tan
all this year—it was almost exactly a year, now, since
Eduard and I had started—but I needed some sun on
my skin. My upper lip had broken out in tiny pimples
like a moustache. Eduard drank his mojito, I drank
my Coke Light. I did not want a drink. We watched
the fat burned white people and ripped Asian boys

and skinny haughty boys in sunglasses. One girl with shoulder-length glossy black hair that hadn't been wet yet stared at Eduard through her aviators. She was standing in the water at the end of the pool with the sun showing on her tight body. Her swimsuit was expensive, red with an orange stripe, and snug. She was drinking cognac from a snifter.

"Do you want to get in the water?" Eduard asked.

"Sure."

I watched him perform in the pool for this young woman. He went underwater and tossed his head back when he came to the surface. He swam laps then stretched his arms and back. He did a backflip off the diving board. I might have done something similar if a beautiful young man were admiring me. Still I was irritated. I stood on a small fountain in the middle of the pool. I was out of the water to about my knees, and I saw that, in the white bikini shorts I had bought, you could see everything.

"Honey," Eduard said. "Come back into the pool. Let me hold you in the water."

"I will," I said. I thought, How do you like it?

He swam to the side and put his sunglasses on. Everyone looks ridiculous when they wear their sunglasses in a swimming pool. But Eduard was wearing his sunglasses in Madonna's swimming pool.

"Maybe we should have bought black shorts for you," Eduard said. He swam back out toward me.

"Or colored ones. The white ones are a little transparent now that they're wet."

I glanced down. "They're fine. You are so paranoid. Besides, you're the one who's showing off."

"Hey, I'm missing you down here," Eduard said. Miss Asian Perfect Body was still watching him. Other people had noticed me. I saw women talking quietly to each other and motioning with their chins the way they do.

I got back into the water. Eduard carried me around the pool.

"You're being silly," I said.

I went and got his mojito from our pool table. Now most of the people there noticed my transparent shorts.

"Pool drinks," I said when I got back to Eduard. It was a joke that Paul used to make.

When we got out of the pool, the couple had taken their deck chairs back.

"Sorry," the man said. The woman regarded me without an expression. Eduard wrapped me in a towel, then put one around himself.

The beautiful young Asian woman hadn't moved from her spot. But now she was eyeing someone else's man.

She'll learn, I thought.

Then I thought, No. As long as there's a market for it, people will always be looking at each other, and enjoying being watched. In the god realm, the Mayans said, they make love by exchanging glances.

Paul's mother told me once, "The worst thing about growing old is that you become invisible." Only a beautiful woman could know something that awful.

TWENTY

I said, "I want to take you out tonight. You're always paying. Let me buy tonight."

"You could buy drinks before dinner. How about that?"

"You choose a place."

He chose the Ritz, which was a good sign. We had made love very gently and for a long time before we went out, and we were happy. We walked along the edge of the sea in the dark. He carried my heels and we held hands. There was no moon, and the water was quiet. From the beach the Ritz-Carleton looked like the nicest hotel in Cancun, but the bar was empty except for three discouraged middle-aged women. They looked like businesspeople or corporate saleswomen of some kind, but there is no business in Cancun.

The pools of the hotel were illuminated and the lights shone across the bar and gave the air an under-water feeling. The women could have been holding their breath, or their gills might have opened, or they could be drowned, I thought. They looked at Eduard with frank appreciation.

It is exhausting dating a sexual man. Every time you walk into a bar or restaurant there they are, all the predators who want to take him from you.

"I want a whiskey," Eduard told the bartender. "With just one cube of ice. She'll have a Coke Light."

The bartender poured him four fingers of whis-key in the glass. I saw him look at the bartender—she was a tiny thing, my size or smaller, she couldn't have weighed ninety pounds—and she moved on down the bar.

It was one of those half-inside-half-outside bars they have at resorts in the tropics.

Eduard took two long sips of his whiskey. He was wearing a linen suit that he knew I loved. I wiped off my lipstick with a cocktail napkin and kissed him.

"I love you," he said. "I really want us to be together."

They were playing old American country music. Eduard finished his drink in three big swallows and ordered another. The bartender poured it the same. He drank it down, and ordered a third.

"What's gotten into you?"

"Let's get in the pool. Come into the pool with me," he said. He got a fourth to carry with him.

"I'll watch you."

"You're no fun," he said.

He took off his shoes, rolled up his trousers to the knee, and walked between the bar pool and the larger infinity pool. The two pools were connected by a shallow, underwater ledge. Walking along it, the water reached Eduard's calves. He took his pants off. He wore yellow silk boxers with elephants printed on them. Both pools were illuminated and the blue light shone up on him from below. He took his shirt off and dipped in the water. The women had perked up. I took pictures with my phone. Eduard took his underwear off, and threw them towards me in a ball. They landed in the pool and floated conspicuously. A husband had arrived and he gave me a questioning look. Even the bartender raised his eyebrows at me.

Eduard was singing in Spanish, in his strong soprano, with his penis flapping around, but he wasn't slurring his words. It was a love song he was singing to the night.

I picked up my Coke Light and moved to a table closer to the pool. It had been raining earlier and I brushed off the cushions before sitting. The cushion soaked the ass of my dress.

"Come on, come out here!" Eduard shouted. I smiled and waved. Just a week ago this would have been the time to drink half of his whiskey, I thought. But I didn't want it.

It may have been stubbornness. No alcoholic, no matter how practiced, whether she's had twenty relapses or never had one in twenty years, can explain why she doesn't take a drink.

He was dancing a tango with himself. I didn't know what I would do if he fell the wrong way. Presumably one of the hotel staff would rescue him. I'd never seen him truly drunk before. He seemed larger. At last he came back to sit with me. He put his clothes back on carefully. He looked around for his underwear, which had at last sunk into the pool. Without getting up, I looked around for his shoes. He walked around barefoot. Then he sat, and quickly stood up again. He wobbled, held the arms of the chair, and sat back down.

"This chair. Got my pants wet." He took a sip of his whiskey. "Did you like my song?"

I showed him the pictures. He laughed. He looked handsome. Drunk and bold and blue in the pool lights and silly. I showed them to him again the next day, performing a post-mortem of my own, and he still loved them.

"Hey, Julio Iglesias," I said, "who's the exhibition-ist now?" And he laughed and said, "What's good for the goose."

We borrowed a convertible from the Mercedes dealer in town—he was a friend of Eduard's—and drove to a house at the end of the peninsula. That night there was a storm and when we woke the ocean and the seaside had been swept clean. The house was down on the sand, and the glass doors of our bedroom opened to the beach and the sea not even fifty yards away.

"Let's get in the ocean," he said.

"Okay, in a minute." No one was up yet. Further down people lived on the beach in little straw huts, and cooked fish, rice and plantains. You could walk across a channel into the grassy jungles of Belize.

Before Cancun, I had told him that everything would be alright with me, again, if I could swim in the ocean with him and see the sun on his skin. When I was sober, this seemed both impossible and true. If I had three drinks I saw it wasn't a dream at all, it was simply going to happen that way, it would all work out, if we were patient, if we could both be kind.

TWENTY-ONE

When we swam the water was too salty and we didn't stay out long. "You're supposed to dive into the waves," he told me.

"I know. I like to swim over them."

When I was a kid in Florida my mom said she liked to watch me go into the surf. I clenched my fists like I wanted to conquer the ocean. I still prefer to stand in the waves and try to jump over them.

The way Eduard swam it was like he was trying to go somewhere.

Like a surfer swims in the ocean, but he wasn't headed for a break.

He held me in his arms, rolling up and down with the forming waves, cradling me and trying to get me to laugh, but it was like we were doing it because we had agreed we would, and it didn't work.

TWENTY-TWO

WE NEVER TOOK A BOAT DOWN TO HONDURAS LIKE we'd planned. We were happy where we were. I did not drink that whole week. But I drank alone, on the flight back to Mexico City. I drank five of those little bottles of wine. The flight attendants are only supposed to give you three, but I charmed mine. When I got off the plane I was elated. I had difficulty with my carry-on bag. In the cab, on the way to my new room at Suenos Realizados, I played Notorious B.I.G. on my iPhone, and discussed the racist lyrics with my

driver, who was Jamaican and, for some reason, did
not seem to mind. In fact, he liked me.

TWENTY-THREE

SADIE TOLD ME A STORY. SHE WAS JUST OUT OF RESI-
dency, and she had divorced her first husband. Her
guru—Sadie's a Buddhist—was coming to Galveston. He wanted to see her, but she did not want to
see him. She did not want to see him because, as she
said, she was "tired of feeling strange." She wanted to
just be a normal person, whatever that is. Her friends
thought having a guru was corny. Sadie wanted to be
like every other Texan psychiatrist, and to go to the
depression conference in Dallas that coincided with

her guru's visit, so that she would have a good excuse to avoid him.

The Buddhist community in Galveston—there is such a thing—was stirred up about it. People were driving down from Houston and Austin to see him speak.

She was ultimately persuaded to stay for her guru. He was staying with a wealthy host in Galveston and the household was being taken care of by several beautiful women from Tyler, Texas. The women of Tyler are as beautiful as one imagines the women from Texas are intended to be.

She was taken to see him in his room. She said for most of her life when she saw her guru, she rarely said anything. On this occasion, she started to cry, because she was divorced, bulimic, and her life seemed chaotic. Also, and more to the point, she cried because she thought she was ugly.

Her guru was quiet for a long time, and then he asked her why she was crying. She was too upset to answer, and she just cried more.

He said, "Do you have a boyfriend?" She shook her head.

"Why don't you have a boyfriend?" he asked.

It occurred to her then that she had been divorced for almost three years.

He said, "Is it because you are sad? They want a happy girlfriend."

She said that she was happy when he told her this, because she knew that it was true.

When I left my first husband for another man, it was only because my husband was sad, and the new man was happy. Every time I walked into the room he lit up. The reason your marriage ends can be that simple.

TWENTY-FOUR

THE YEAR WAS COMING TO AN END.

"Where should we go for New Year's?"

"Nicaragua," I said. Paul had taken me there before we were married. I wanted to see what it would look like, now, with my new eyes. And if it looks the same, I thought, maybe I'm meant to be back with Paul.

In Leon we stayed at a perfumerie with only one guest room. The high ceilings had beams, there was a chandelier over the freestanding tub and another chandelier over the four-poster bed, and the sun porch looked down on the little main street of the town. There was not much to do and we had too much time to talk. Whenever we knew we should be talking we had sex.

We were downstairs having coffee. The woman who ran the perfumerie made the coffee and Eduard invited her to sit with us. She was an American who had fallen in love with a local boy and now they were having a baby.

"The owners wanted to invite you to their home for New Year's Eve," she said. "It's their other hotel, at the ruins. It will be a nice group."

The owners were both former models, an Argentinian and an Italian.

I didn't want to go but I knew that Eduard did, so I agreed.

"Did you see how disappointed she was?" I asked Eduard. "She wanted to be invited to the dinner party."

"I don't think so. I think she wanted to stay in town and watch the fireworks with her family," Eduard said.

"Maybe so."

It was funny, I thought, that his account of what the manager wanted to do was just what I wanted to do, and vice versa. I don't know which one of us was right. But it was characteristic of us that we assigned to other people the motivations and desires we suspected in each other.

TWENTY-FIVE

THE HOTEL BY THE RUINS, WHERE THE MODELS LIVED, was an hour from Leon. We found it as the sun was setting. It was next to a small lake but there were no mosquitoes because it was winter. A bonfire was burning and you could hear the occasional splash of a crocodile in the lake. The table was set for twelve.

We met the host and his wife.

"Eduard," she said. "I'm so glad you came. My husband told me about you two."

Her husband was often in and out of the perfumerie. We had seen him several times, sometimes with a very beautiful Czech model who was clearly strung out on heroin. I could see the husband and the junkie were having an affair. The shockingly beautiful junkie was at the dinner with her boyfriend, a musician. But she could barely hold her head up.

"I'm sorry," the host's wife said to me. She was sitting next to Eduard and her face was a bit too close. She had a lovely Italian accent and had recently had a baby. I was intimidated, and she was watching me carefully.

The host's wife said to me, "I think I don't remember your name?"

"Her name is Brett," Eduard jerked forward. "It's strange. It's a boy's name."

The hostess leaned across Eduard and shook my hand. "Happy New Year," she said.

TWENTY-SIX

Through dinner Eduard sat rigidly while the other couples relaxed and held each other. When I tried to touch him he pulled away.

"You see how they are together? That's how normal couples act," I told Eduard quietly. He didn't respond.

The owner's three-year-old daughter was still up, and she played and threw herself on her parents. I thought about Paul's boys.

Eduard was drinking white wine and I kept refilling his glass. I thought he might relax and enjoy himself. It was a New Year's Eve party. We should try to have fun.

When I went to the bathroom I saw bottles of wine on a stand and I took one to the bathroom with me. I used a nail file to push the cork in and hid it in a cabinet under the sink. I checked my teeth to make sure they weren't purple from the red wine.

We were a hit at the party—I put on the best show I could, to prove to Eduard that I belonged. The junkie's boyfriend and I talked about Almodovar movies, impressing each other. In a slightly different life, I thought, it might just as well have been this one.

When we left Eduard was happy. He'd had a nice time. He was drunk and had his arm around me, and was laughing. We were imitating people at the party the way we liked to. They'd invited us to spend the night, but I whispered in his ear: "Can you imagine waking up to these people?"

In the jeep, before we drove off, I turned to him and said, "Her name is Brett. It's a silly name. It's a boy's name."

TWENTY-SEVEN

WE FOUGHT THAT NIGHT—WE MISSED THE FIRE-
works—and all the next day, between having sex and
me hurrying off "to buy a Coke Light." I was doing
shots of tequila at a bar a couple of blocks from our
place. Then we drove south, to the very southern
end of the country, and had four tranquil nights in a
guesthouse owned by some ex-pats in a town so small
that no one knows it's there. It is hidden in a wildlife
preserve and the other guests were marine biologists
from California who swam a mile in the ocean every

morning, and had come to snorkel and scuba dive on the reef.

We took a kayak out. We saw a sea turtle in the water and we tried to keep up with it in our kayak. Every time I thought it had disappeared he found it again hiding near one of the many little reefs and coral buds. We went a long way out, trying to reach a point that was miles from our hotel—I knew we'd be lucky if we made it halfway—and stopped on a deserted beach, and walked for a while, and looked in tide pools. I wanted to show him an octopus hiding. On one beach a woman came out and told us we had to move our kayak, and then we saw that it was a small hotel, and the beach was nude. The woman was loud and rude because she thought we had come to look at naked people. But there was no one but us anywhere you looked. We held hands as we walked and we kissed and I wondered if I should make love to him in some hidden spot—I had often made love to Paul in the sand, and it had always been awkward and fun—but I was tired and I didn't want to. When we were back in the water I asked Eduard if he could do the paddling for a while and I lay back and closed my eyes with a towel under my head. When I asked if he wanted help getting us back to the house he flexed his bicep for me and I laughed. The tide was against us and the sun was going down so after half an hour or so I started paddling again.

We made it back just as the sun set. He pulled the kayak up and lifted it into its wooden stand. I leaned the paddles against the side of the house. We had sex in the hammock.

"This has been the only place I really like in Nicaragua," he said. "I liked all our places," I lied. "But this was my favorite."

TWENTY-EIGHT

EDUARD HAD MOVED OUT OF HIS CONDO AND bought a house. He was having a housewarming party. I wasn't invited.

"I already bought my ticket. I'm going to be in town. If you want me to stay with you I will. Or if you want some space I'll stay in a hotel."

"Of course you're staying with me," Eduard said. "I'm excited that you're coming. I'm just not ready to make a public announcement that we're a couple."

"Everybody already knows, Eduard. All of your friends know more than I would have told them, if I lived there. You're the one who talks."

"I'm not ready for you to meet Grace and Reynaldo."

They were a famous couple in Panama, in their seventies, real money—Reynaldo's father had supplied the concrete when they built the canal. They were both recovered alcoholics. They had been friends of Eduard's for years and were like parents to Eduard. They had tried to make him stay at their place during the breakup with Lurisia. I had the impression that they thought well of me. When Eduard quoted them back to me they were usually speaking in my defense, or at least in defense of the possibility of our relationship. Unlike his other friends, who always seemed to me to insist that we were doomed.

"All of my friends think you're a falling down drunk."

"Eduard, please. All of your friends are falling down drunks."

He was quiet for a minute. Then he said, "You're right. Fair enough. Except Grace and Reynaldo. It's true. They are all alcoholics. It's not like you'd be the only drunk there."

"And Grace and Reynaldo understand. They quit drinking for a reason."

"I know."

He was good about that. If I disagreed with him, he'd listen, think it through, and if he were wrong, he'd revise his opinion. There aren't many people like that.

In fact most people are just the opposite. The more you disagree with them, the more committed they become to the lie they're telling you, or themselves, or the both of you.

There was something Eduard wasn't telling me. I asked him if Lurisia was coming to the party and he said, "I doubt it. But it would be fine if she were. She'll bring her new boyfriend." She had started dating a poet. I supposed they had met in her clinic.

TWENTY-NINE

I FLEW DOWN. WE CHRISTENED THE HOUSE. THE DAY of the party Eduard was meeting a potential for lunch. He was a very successful developer and he was considering moving from his banker to Eduard. This was the man who would renovate all the hotels in Cuba, when it finally happened, and build the new ones. He had already signed a contract for the Peninsula Havana, and a Four Seasons Resort outside Santiago de Cuba.

"Just stay in bed," he told me. "I've got to hurry."

I wouldn't let him out of bed until we'd had sex several times, and finally he stopped us and said, "Really. I can't be late for this."

"I'll come with you."

"You can't come with me."

"Not to the lunch, dummy. I'll ride in the cab and work while you're at your lunch. You can meet me after."

We still hadn't figured out whether I could come to his party, or where I was going to spend the night if I wasn't invited. After a year of hiding things from each other and the people around us, it was a habit. We could leave something unspoken right until the moment of crisis.

When we got out of the cab I kissed him and wished him good luck.

We agreed to meet at a pizza place we both liked after his lunch.

He hurried away, walking that "important businessman" walk of his that he walked sometimes and didn't suit him.

I found a restaurant to have a coffee. It was a nice place and they were empty except for me. The owner was opening wine bottles for his waitstaff to try, so they would know what to recommend, and he offered me a glass. I accepted, and he continued to offer me glasses from each new bottle. I warned him that my guest was arriving soon, and I didn't want him to know I had been drinking. He avoided me after that, and a waiter brought me a glass of water.

When Eduard came, I was drunk.

He told me the developer wanted to do business. He looked at me. I looked back at him and smiled. I didn't bother to try to hide the fact that I was drunk, or to lie about it. I shrugged.

"So I've been thinking, and I'd like a thirty day break," he said. He sat down. He paused. "I mean, Brett, what am I supposed to say at this point?"

"It's over," I said. "We don't need a break."

I wouldn't have had the courage to say what we both knew was true if I hadn't been drunk.

The waiter came. I ordered him a glass of champagne to celebrate his new client. They'd promote him to senior partner for this one. They'd give him a piece of the bank.

"You may as well have a glass, too," he said.

I ordered a second glass. We toasted. He took a sip of his wine, and then put down his glass and said, "I can't do this, Brett." He walked out. I looked at the champagne and realized I didn't want it either. But I sat there and drank the two glasses and paid the check.

THIRTY

MIGUEL'S ON HERMOSA OPENS AT 11 A.M. AND WAS walking distance from the library. It was under new management so they didn't know me from the old days and wouldn't chase me away. The bartender poured me real drinks. I had five vodka sodas and I don't remember leaving the bar. I had to meet a real estate agent about a house I wanted to rent. During the walk I realized how drunk I was and I called Sadie.

"Tell me honestly," I said. "You can hear I'm having a bit of trouble." She made that kind noise she makes.

"I have a meeting. About a house. It's important. I have to have a house. I promised Paul. Do you think I can go?"

"I think maybe you should skip it this time. Are you going to be okay? Do you want me to call you a ride home?"

"No, I'm okay. I'm supposed to already have the house today. I'm supposed to take his boys tonight."

"Maybe you could take a nap? Brett, I think you should text Paul to change the day, then go back to the hotel and lie down for a bit."

"Sadie. Usually if someone's in a bad situation, they don't want the truth."

I went to the bar at The Raphael. I had to pick up the boys at Paul's at five. I found out later that they bounced me from The Raphael bar that afternoon.

When I checked back into the hotel a few weeks later my favorite bartender told me, after I apologized: "That's fine. But I can't serve you down here anymore. It's from the management. You'll have to use your mini-bar." He was stern and I wondered if I'd taken off my clothes or invited him up to my room. I have lost bartenders that way before.

THIRTY-ONE

I REMEMBER PARTS OF THE DRIVE TO GET THE BOYS. The auto parts store on El Novio and Hermosa. Telling myself not to take a left there. The red light and the cop who waved at me while everyone honked. An Outkast song on the radio. I was elated and turned it up. Headed the wrong way on a one-way side street near Paul's house and trying to do a three-point turn, then giving up and taking the straightest way.

I don't remember arriving at the house, or how I convinced Bella to leave, or what game or movie I started playing for them. Thinking back on it now, I expect they were hungry for dinner. Or maybe Bella had made something.

Bella called Paul, and I do remember when he got to the house. I think I asked him not to shout in front of the boys. I can remember him putting me in his car. He told me I had been lying down in the kitchen with macaroni and cheese boiling over on the stove.

"I want to spend the night here!" I screamed, and Paul said, "Brett, you are not well right now." His ten-year-old stood silently, immobile, in the front door of the house. He was following his father's requests carefully and quickly. The sunlight was bright and Paul wouldn't listen to anything I said. "I'm okay," I told him. "Please let me stay. Yes I had a couple of drinks. But let me stay. Paul, please let me stay. I just want to stay."

THIRTY-TWO

AFTER PAUL DROPPED ME AT THE RAPHAEL I RAN A
hot bath. I called room service and asked for a shaving razor and a bottle of scotch. I took all my valium,
broke the bit of razor out of the plastic, and called
Eduard. The veins were slippery little devils and with
the sliver of razor I was only able to get the ones on
my left wrist. It's harder than it looks. I cut the thumb
and fingers of my right hand doing it.

When we got off the phone Eduard called Paul,
and soon, as the water was turning pink and all the
light in the room seemed to go pink along with it,

Paul and the manager came in the bathroom, and they lifted me up out of the tub like I was a bubble and carried me to the hospital.

THIRTY-THREE

WHEN EDUARD WAS STILL LIVING WITH LURISIA, WE were walking in Panama City, in the shade in a park, under the purple trees, holding hands, and he said: "I enjoy living a double life. I don't want to face the truth." He was being playful but he meant it. I said, "That's almost exactly what Anna Karenina says."

The illusions we depended on about love and each other were necessary to keep us going. Yes, it all collapsed. But afterwards, I think we both wondered, will I ever have something that good again?

ABOUT THE AUTHOR

Clancy Martin is the author of the award-winning novel *How To Sell*, the philosophical memoir *Love and Lies*, as well as many books in philosophy, and has translated Friedrich Nietzsche, Søren Kierkegaard, and others. A Guggenheim Fellow and a contributing editor at *Harper's* and *Vice*, his work has been translated into more than thirty languages. He teaches philosophy in Kansas City, Missouri, where he lives with his wife the writer Amie Barrodale, his two youngest daughters. Margaret and Portia, and his unruly Labradoodle, Simha Mukha.

ACKNOWLEDGMENTS

My deepest thanks to the gracious and patient monks and other Buddhist friends at the Kungri Monastery in the Pin Valley, India, where this manuscript was first written; to Wayne and the gang at UMKC; to Tim Small, the kind editor who first conceived of, motivated and published the project overseas; to Lorin Stein and my all-knowing, all-good agent Susan Golomb, who together convinced me to rewrite what began as a memoir into fiction; to my brilliant editor Giancarlo DiTrapano, who has been relentless in his determination to see it appear here in the US, and who has quite possibly put as much passion into the book as I have; to Mom, Alicia, Rebecca, Darren, Pat and Mompat; to Rinpoche; and above all, to my daughters, Zelly, Margaret and Portia, and to my best reader, best friend, and loving wife, Amie.

Lydia Cassatt Reading the Morning Paper

Lydia Cassatt Reading the Morning Paper

Harriet Scott Chessman

<u>C</u>

CENTURY

Published by Century in 2003

1 3 5 7 9 10 8 6 4 2

First published in the United Kingdom in 2003 by Century

The Random House Group Limited
20 Vauxhall Bridge Road, London SW1V 2SA

Random House Australia (Pty) Limited
20 Alfred Street, Milsons Point, Sydney,
New South Wales 2061, Australia

Random House New Zealand Limited
18 Poland Road, Glenfield
Auckland 10, New Zealand

Random House South Africa (Pty) Limited
Endulini, 5a Jubilee Road, Parktown 2193, South Africa

The Random House Group Limited Reg. No. 954009

www.randomhouse.co.uk

A CIP catalogue record for this book
is available from the British Library

Papers used by Random House are natural, recyclable
products made from wood grown in sustainable forests.
The manufacturing processes conform to the environmental
regulations of the country of origin.

ISBN 0 7126 2363 9

Typeset by MATS, Southend-on-Sea, Essex
Printed and bound in Great Britain by
Biddles Ltd, Guildford and King's Lynn

The imperfect is our paradise.

—Wallace Stevens, "The Poems of Our Climate"

To M. Lucia Kuppens, O.S.B.
and the Abbey of Regina Laudis

and to the memory of
Shirley Martin Prown

Recordáre

This story is based on the lives of the American Impressionist painter Mary Cassatt (1844–1926) and her sister Lydia Cassatt (1837–1882). Each of the five chapters centers around one of Mary's paintings of Lydia. I have attempted to be as accurate as possible about the Cassatts' lives, yet this is most definitely a work of fiction. The paintings themselves, so moving and appealing, have drawn me to the figure of Lydia, painted again and again by her sister. I have thought, imagined, and dreamt my way into her world.

CHAPTERS

1. *Woman Reading* 1

2. *Tea* 39

3. *The Garden* 75

4. *Driving* 105

5. *Lydia Seated at an Embroidery Frame* 135

xi

Woman Reading

In my dream, I walk down the five flights of stairs to the avenue in Paris, yet when I open the heavy front door, I am on the porch at Hardwicke. Robbie is pulling May in a wagon on the pebbled drive, and out in the meadow, I know, Aleck is already beginning to urge his horse over the jumps. The day is bright, and I run toward the barn to saddle up Juno, when suddenly

i.

"Could you model for me tomorrow, Lyd?"

May's looking at me with a kind of urgency and hopefulness. I've been showing her some new dress patterns, as we linger at the table after breakfast. She looks sweet for a moment, and worried, and I say, "I think so."

"Mother thinks it will make you too tired."

"Yes, I do," calls Mother, from her room.

"*N'importe quoi*. I'm so much better now."

I drink my coffee, picturing the walk to May's studio. It's only a few streets away, just off the place Pigalle, but I haven't been well, and in any case I've become attached to this perch, our apartment on avenue Trudaine, in the *9ème arrondissement*. We're in Paris, and yet we're also in our own world, five stories up; we've become a bit like a nation, The Cassatt Nation, small and besieged, at times, and independent. In the kitchen, the new maid Lise is clattering the

5

dishes. Father rustles the paper in the parlor; he's been reading us bits out of *Le Petit Parisien*.

I rise to look out the window. Over the tops of the apartments across from us, I see the white and cream buildings scrambling up the hill of Montmartre, among trees and gardens. Looking down to the avenue Trudaine, I see a girl in a royal blue coat and a red hat race along the street with a dog. I'm in love with all of this, this bright and foreign life.

"I could have the carriage brought round, Lyddy."

"Such a short distance, May! Don't be silly!"

"The carriage is a good idea," Mother says, coming into the dining room. She's wearing her specs and her old white morning gown, with her light wool shawl. How old she's begun to look, I think.

I know May needs me to model. It's partly the cost, of course, to hire someone else. To pay a model—well, it adds up, and Father's at her constantly now about making her way, and covering all of her own expenses, for the studio too. "Think for yourself, May," he said this morning, as we sat down to breakfast, "think what this costs us, and tally up your sales this year. Got to consider this."

I glimpse two young men on the avenue, elegantly dressed, talking and gesturing energetically as they stroll. I open the long window and lean over the small *balcon* for a moment, to catch a better look.

6

Perhaps May knows them? Maybe they're on their way to one of the cafés at the place Pigalle, to smoke cigarettes, and drink coffee, and argue about art. I see such men, often, sitting outside a café like Degas' favorite, Le Rat Mort. Women too go there; sometimes, as I walk with May, I see mothers and grandmothers sitting happily, with pretty children, eating sliced melon or apricot pie.

Once I saw a woman sitting close to a young man. I glimpsed him nuzzling her, kissing her neck, and, before I could look away, I caught the expression on her face, a mixture of coolness and knowledge and pleasure.

"I think I'll go to the Bois today, give your horse some exercise," Father says cheerfully to May.

I look over May's shoulder. She's studying a pattern I chose at Worth's, for an evening gown with an off-the-shoulder *décolleté*.

"It would look delicious on you, in a yellow silk," I say.

May looks up. I can see she's studying me with her painter's eyes. Inwardly, I flinch; I feel shy, always, when someone looks at me. She's my younger sister, by a full seven years, I remind myself, even if she's thirty-four now, and yet I feel so much younger than May sometimes. I can't help wondering what she sees. I'm as plain as a loaf of bread.

As if divining my thoughts, May smiles. She peels an orange with a little knife. "You can look away. You can be reading this time."

7

"Ah, yes." I smile as I sit down across the table from her. May knows me well, for within this Cassatt Nation, my own small acre has treasures of books stashed everywhere, in the elbows of trees, beneath berry bushes, on benches by streams. My little house is composed of books: English and French novels, and books of poetry too, gold-edged. I, who am moderate in so much, who bend myself to family life, am most immoderate once I'm in my acre. I read for hours, with passion, ardently wishing the stone wall around me to hold, the little gate to feel the pressure of no hand, the latch to grow rusty.

"I wish we had brought more of that honey back to Paris from the country," Mother says, her specs slipping down her nose. She's writing a list for Lise's shopping today.

"I'm sure we can find good honey somewhere in Paris," May says drily. "You didn't have any orange this morning, Lyddy, did you?" she asks, holding out a section of hers. The peelings make a sphere on her plate.

I accept the orange sliver.

"Maybe you can just do the back of my head," I suggest.

"*Mais non*, Lyddy. I want your lovely face."

She looks at me teasingly, and *for a moment I am riding in the country again, in West Chester, Pennsylvania. It's early spring, snow still on the*

8

ground in places, and we must have been back from our long stay in Europe for a year or so. We had buried Robbie in Germany. I picture myself riding with Aleck and his friend from Yale, Thomas Houghton. The day is chilly, and, once we've dismounted, I take off my gloves and rub my hands together, holding them to my mouth. Thomas is close to me. "Cold?" he asks, catching my hands in his, chafing, bringing them halfway to his mouth.

"How about a profile?" May asks.

"If it helps you out, May, yes."

"You're helping me immensely. We'll begin tomorrow morning."

I think of the quiet day tomorrow would have been, West Chester swirled away into the past now, along with Philadelphia and Pittsburgh, my life a new one here in Paris, talking to Mother and Father, reading a novel, looking through my patterns, hoping through it all to make some miraculous leap out of my condition, to become healthy again. I contemplate the slow descent down five flights to the avenue, and the slow walk by May's side, through a late September morning. I prefer the longer journey, along avenue Trudaine to the park at the place d'Anvers, because of the trees, the green island. Then up we walk to the busy boulevard de Rochechouart and the boulevard de Clichy, coming at last to the place Pigalle, my body increasingly assaulted and aroused by a myriad of things: the trolleys, the laborers, the shop assistants, the pavements in front of cafés still damp from being washed, the scent of coffee and bread, and of manure too.

"Tomorrow morning, yes," I say, feeling worried but brave, and picturing my little boat, leaks and all, bobbing along in the wake of my sister's grander vessel, sailing to Heaven knows where.

ii.

I sink into the plump green chair in May's studio, holding the paper.

After breakfast this morning, Mother asked me a dozen times if I really felt well enough, demanding that May paint only for an hour, or at most two. As I put on my bonnet and gloves, Father too began to fret. "Are you warm, Lyddy?" he asked. "Make sure she stands up to stretch, at least every half-hour, May." Then he called to Lise to "bring Mademoiselle Cassatt's slippers, and—what about a small pillow?" After all this fuss, as always, I questioned the entire idea of modeling. If I became exhausted before I arrived at the door of our apartment, how could I possibly think of helping May?

I listen to the city's constant clatter and clamor outside the windows of May's studio, and I think of the shops we passed this morning, so much more seductive, even in this gritty district, than those I remember in the States. Each shop window lures me with something delicious or fine: *prâlines*, cut flowers, linens and silks. "It makes America look pretty bare, doesn't it?" May said to me last week, and she's right, in a sense. Certainly shops like the ones near the new Opéra and the Tuileries amaze the wealthiest of our American friends. All of them flock to the Bon Marché too, and the other *grands magasins*, filled, layer after layer, like the inside of wedding cakes, with things to buy. Philadelphia can't compare, and yet I sometimes miss those modest shops. Something appeals to me in restraint.

Le Petit Journal becomes absurdly heavy in my hands, and my arms ache. I've read all the articles, and editorial opinions, and advertisements too, and now I'm wishing I had my book. "Women are always pictured reading books," May said, as we set up this morning. "A newspaper is perfect. And what could be better than *Le Petit Journal*? It's so modern. It shows you're a thinking woman." I yearn, though, for the novel I began yesterday and left sitting on my bed—*Madame Bovary*. I'm reading it for the second time, and I relish it even more now than I did when I was younger.

As I pose, I remember how Mother loved sitting for her portrait last spring. She would make light of her contribution—"All I do is lounge in a soft chair and read the paper," she'd say, waving her hand—but she would seem happier than usual, as if she had been granted a second life in the studio, more carefree, more glamorous, than this one. Father's irritations and demands seemed to reach her only through a haze. "Yes, my dear," she would say happily, "I'll be sure to come home tomorrow well in time for lunch," or "Of course I'll write to Aleck and to Gardner tomorrow."

When I first saw Mother's picture, the painting seemed reckless, May's brushstrokes bold, Mother's *déshabillé* a harum-scarum wash of colors. I felt wonder, and jealousy too. This shimmer, this feeling—how under Heaven had she created this? The painting showed Mother, simply herself, with her specs, reading the paper as on any ordinary morning. Yet May had caught a feeling, a whole moment, in paint. It was every bit as striking as Berthe Morisot's pictures, and more appealing to me than any of the ones I'd seen by May's other new friends, even Renoir.

How courageous May had become! To paint the ordinary,

a woman in her morning dress reading *Le Figaro*, and to make the picture dance like this, to feel unbound by all the things one had been taught, or by the paintings put up each spring at the Salon, so dark and classical. Mother praised May's painting in her offhand manner—"Lovely light, don't you think, Lyddy, and look how May used the mirror!"—but I knew she felt proud.

iv.

Around the rectangle of *Le Petit Journal*, the parquet floors of May's studio shine. I can see the edge of one of her Turkish rugs, the rose and gray one, in intricate patterns. My arms and shoulders feel sore.

"A cup of tea, Lyddy?"

"Thanks, yes."

"I've made you pose for over an hour. Mother would be furious."

As I put the newspaper down, tiny pinpricks run into my fingers. The little gold hands on the clock above the mantel say half past ten.

May moves about the studio with her usual quickness. She darts, like a bird. She's slender, almost too thin, really. As she opens the tin of tea, I think of Mother, when she was younger and healthier, making tea for us on Sundays, wherever we lived, and I picture May too, as a little girl on a pony, her face stubborn and shining. *"Let me try,"* she's saying to Aleck and me, as Robbie looks on from the gate. She's four or so, and I must be about eleven, Aleck nine, and how old would Robbie be? Seven? We're in the meadow by our country house, Hardwicke, before our move to Philadelphia. Aleck and I love to jump our horses, small jumps. The meadow at Hardwicke's just been mown, and the ground is uneven. Robbie swings on the gate, and *"Let me try,"* she *says again. "You're too little," Aleck says, but in a moment she's in the air, her small figure rising inches above her pony's back, and soon she's jumping, again, and again, and Aleck shouts, "Good jumping, Mame!" and I shout, "Careful!" I'm angry with her, because she never listens. At dinner that night, when I begin to tell the story, May and Robbie interrupt, and then Father says she should have lessons with us if she's so bent on jumping.*

As May brings me my tea, she reminds me of a mermaid; something about her floats, skims the waves. For a moment I wonder what it would be like to be an artist. How does a woman make such a choice? Or is it something that comes to one, like a gift from heaven?

"Et bien, you look thoughtful, Lyd."

I smile, brushing the air in front of my nose as if to say, It's nothing. Sipping my tea, walking about May's studio, I study some of her pictures: a woman holding out a treat for a dog, a woman reading, sketches of Mother by the lamp at home. I come upon one of May's self-portraits too, the little gouache on paper, and think how much more striking it is than some of the other pictures, and how odd she looks in it, not quite like herself. She appears serious and jaunty, leaning hard into a green cushion. Her dress is lovely, the white one Madame Ange made for her, but her face looks sad, and stubborn too.

Bold she is, and not like other women.

"Do you like this one?" May is at my shoulder.

"I do. Well, 'like' may not be the right word."

"No?"

"I find it formidable."

"Well, I don't mind being formidable!" May slips her arm through mine.

"Yes, and I admire the dress too."

"You helped me find the material for that dress, Lyddy, *tu te souviens?*"

It occurs to me that May has in this self-portrait an air of someone looked at—looked at by someone else, I mean, and not me, or Mother. I think of Degas. She's with him so much now, and certainly she admires his painting immensely, and she's learned from him, about color, and angle, and brushwork, and capturing the ordinary life.

The picture holds more than all this, though; it's as if May painted it as he looked over her shoulder.

As I sink into the green chair again, taking up *le journal*, May says, "You look splendid today, you know, Lyd."

"Thank you. Maybe it's your eyes."

"*Mais non*, anyone would agree with me, Lyddy. You've always been beautiful."

As I find my pose, I think about how, when I first met Degas, he gave me the impression of an intelligent but fierce dog—well-dressed and utterly *comme il faut*, but a dog nonetheless. He bit into subjects—the foolishness of one artist or another, the insipidity of someone's latest effort, I can't remember—and all the while his eyes lit on things in our apartment, with an air of studying and maybe breaking them: the tea set, the Japanese vase on the mantel, me. I felt sure that if I opened my mouth, he would pounce. It's a kind of brutality.

And yet, something else emerged as he asked me questions. "Had I begun to feel better?" he asked, and "What was I reading?" When I told him, "Jane Austen," he looked curious. "Ah, *lequel*?" "*Persuasion*," I said, and then, surprisingly, his eyes lit on mine. A feeling connected

16

us, quickly and with an absorbing depth. I wondered what he felt. In allowing myself to look at his face, which had seemed so arrogant and almost ugly a moment before, I discovered a sadness, maybe, or a sense of pain. It was as if I had rounded a corner, in a strange city, and had come upon a scene of terrible intimacy: a man weeping, a child ill. Yet, before I could think of something to say, the city rose up before me again, with its elegant avenues and public spaces, its overwhelming buildings, looming, sharp-edged.

I wonder about May, for she seems to welcome his presence. Certainly, he seems to have made of her—and of me too—an exception, and yet this sensation of being protected from the Cyclops by the Cyclops himself, while he eats everyone else in sight—well, it's fragile at best. And he does eat people, I know, one friend after another.

And yet I could see what he meant to her, from the beginning. His invitation to her, a year ago, to join his group of Independents, came to her as an invitation to live, to create the art she knew she could create. Her whole desire now is to have her début in the Impressionist Exhibition this spring.

At tea, on that first meeting, I saw something else. In the air between him and May, I sensed something bright and resonant. She smiled, and he bent toward her.

In May's studio, my arms ache again. May and I have been quiet for some time. I catch myself almost sleeping when May's voice cuts into the drowsy air.

"I might go to the Louvre this afternoon, Lyddy. Could you come too?"

"I'd love to, if I feel able."

"We could look at the Dutch collection again."

"*Oui.*"

"Maybe May Alcott will come with us. We can go by carriage, and fetch her."

May Alcott, Louisa May Alcott's sister, is married to a Swiss man now, so we see her much less, but I welcome our outings with her, and with our young and wealthy friend Louisine Elder. To go about Paris with this small crowd makes me feel young and careless, or, as careless as I can be.

Love comes, or illness. Last summer, my life changed, all in a day. After asking me questions, with his little pince-nez glittering, the doctor took May and Father aside to discuss my situation. Mother was ill then. When May returned to my room, her face a map of worry, I knew in a moment how bad it was, and I knew too how she would fight this truth, how everyone would fight it. I could not hear all of her words, because the world seemed to become unreal, as if I were miles away, looking through the small end of a telescope, just as I used to do with Robbie's when he got a toy one for Christmas one winter at Hardwicke. I would sit in the window seat, behind the curtains, and point the instrument out to the meadow, and at first I could see the horses so clearly that I could watch the breath coming out of their nostrils, and then I'd turn the telescope around, and suddenly the meadows, and the road, and May's snow castle, and the flower garden—dry sticks in snow now—would become tiny, a perfect miniature. Only this time, when May spoke, the miniature held her and me and my bed, in my room in Paris, and all around the world had vanished, and I felt myself too to have no substance, but to be made of air. Pain and air.

"Bright's Disease," she said, and I almost laughed, thinking how ridiculous that a disease of the kidneys should be associated in any way with brightness. "But, Lyddy, even a French doctor can be wrong. We must simply watch your diet, and keep you well rested. That's all there is to it. You must simply be careful."

But how can carefulness make this all right? It's not up to me. Heaven knows, I'm nothing if not careful. This illness is inside me. I feel that I live on a plank jutting out over an ocean filled with sea monsters. Sometimes I think I'm better. But maybe it's just that a pavilion has been created around my little plank, right by this ocean, sea monsters or no, and so much goes on in it—jugglers, singers, romance—that I am merely distracted and amused.

"Lyddy, did you hear me?"

"*Désolée*, I must be daydreaming."

"I can tell! I have to pull you back, Lyd, right back into that chair. You left me quite alone there, for a few minutes. Where did you travel to?"

I smile. "Oh, well, I go anywhere I wish, May: Pennsylvania, Germany . . ."

"Not Germany!"

"Actually, I was probably thinking simply about our apartment, and lunch."

"Lunch can be an absorbing subject, I know."

"Yes, and that pattern for a new gown."

"Another absorbing subject."

I can't always tell May my thoughts, because she can't bear to face illness or death. My whole family's like that.

I think May's sadness, when she heard my diagnosis, was increased by her memory of earlier sorrows. The doctor, even,

Woman Reading (Femme lissant), Joslyn Art Museum, Omaha, Nebraska.

may have reminded her of other doctors, like the fat German one in Darmstadt, who looked at Robbie's legs, and told us there was nothing seriously wrong with him. All we had to do, he said, was to make Robbie exercise with regularity, and take some medicine to strengthen his bones. For awhile we could all look at each other as if the world were an ordinary place.

But if something comes to someone, and makes of their body a house to waste and gnaw at, doctors can do nothing, and love can do nothing either. The baby, George, died too, only a month old, when May was just beginning to walk, and, before I was born, the baby girl, Katherine, named for Mother. Once the youngest, Gardner, came into the world, three years after George, I could hardly bear to look at him, for fear he too would be still and cold.

"I think that'll do for today," May says. I can tell she's pleased with her start.

I rouse myself, and shake off my thoughts. To be in May's studio, now, in Paris, and not in Darmstadt, or in Pennsylvania either—to have come this far—well, it's lucky.

"May I see?" I ask.

"It's only a start," she says, and I look at a swath of white paint—the *fichu* around my shoulders—and the beginnings of a

woman's face, in profile, the nose and mouth painted with deli-
cacy, the eye a darker line, and a sketchy band of brown for her
hair, whitish-pink broad strokes for her cap.

Something about this woman, half-suggested in oil, makes me
bend toward her. *Who is this?* I ask myself, for I can't think it is I,
and yet I know, with exquisite pleasure, that it is.

vi.

As I sit in my armchair, reading Flaubert, later, the image of this
woman, the one May is painting, comes to me again and again. I
discover a yearning to be close to her, to be present as she comes
closer to the surface. It's like watching someone swim toward you,
only it's much slower, and you see her at first underwater, a moving blur, and you wait for the moment when you'll see her arms,
and then her face, her hair streaming wet in the light.

I could never confess this to anyone, and I can barely even think it,
but I'm aware too of another sensation, the feeling of May's eyes
on me, as she painted this morning. Do other women have such
feelings? It isn't that I feel beautiful. It isn't something outward or
visible, really, at all.

Such sensations make me think of my girlhood. I look closely at each memory, in my own gallery, as if to discover some clue, some fresh element in the story: a hand on an arm, a glance, a glove left on a seat, maybe. It still surprises me that I never married.

Of course marriage isn't the solution to all of life's ills. It can bring boatfuls of ills, if one is unlucky—think how unhappy people can be, yoked together. That's what I admire about Flaubert, how he sees that, and makes even the dullest marriage into an interesting story. He creates poor Emma Bovary, full of restlessness and vague dreams, romantic wishes, and here she is (I'm halfway through), caught in life's meshes already, an absurd marriage, an impossible love affair.

How does one go about this business of living? I dwell on this question often, now. One's life looks different, terribly sharp and clear, when one begins to comprehend the fact of one's very particular, looming death.

vii.

Sitting in front of the mirror in my nightgown, brushing my hair, I look younger than I feel, as always, although I can see, these days, hints of the old woman I might become, if I'm lucky. I study my fine crows' feet, the shadows under my eyes. My hair, in waves, looks reddish blonde still in this lamplight; only in the day can I see the change, especially at my temples, to white.

In bed, with the lamp out, I find myself remembering the War at home. It still feels fresh to me, the tearing up of our cousins' land in Gettysburg, the long and bloody list of young men who entered the fight: John Chandler, James Endicott, Andrew Lyman, handsome William Dabney. At least Robbie was spared such a challenge. And when I heard of another death, of some- one young and fine, I felt another door close inside me, a breeze blowing it shut. I had written letters to each of them, attempting to sound cheerful, as if the world had not opened up a hideous wound, and as if they were not positioned to fall, limbs blown off, chests yawning red, their horses foundering in the mud. We urged Aleck to hire a substitute, and thank God he did, or he too might be bones, like our cousin Frank. It isn't fair, Heaven knows, and Aleck will carry the knowledge with him all his life, but look at him now, vice president of the Pennsylvania Railroad, with wealth and a full, rich life, a country house, a fine marriage, four children.

And Thomas Houghton, whose eyes were the color of hazel, and who almost brought my hands to his mouth, who kissed me one summer night in West Chester, moulders now beneath Pennsylvania soil.

All those lives, all those lives, and I felt my life too whisked away, in the shot of a cannon, the tearing apart of flesh from bone, heart from rib, my brains blown and scattered into a thousand pieces, the green fields turned to blood and muck, my life over at twenty-seven, for how was I to live, then? To live, afterward, I thought at first, was to walk always on graves, hearing the whisper of ghosts. Not Robbie's ghost only, now, or the babies', but thousands of others too, and in my dreams each night I'd see a meadow of men, mowed down, moaning, and I'd look into the face of each, searching for one face, and sometimes I would find that face only to see it crumble, or shatter, before I could touch it.

I wake frightened, and for one wild moment, seeing only dark, I have no idea where I am: *in the root cellar at Hardwicke? In Germany? In West Chester? In the new house we built in the country, when I was twenty-three? In Allegheny City, when I was little? Yes, in Allegheny City, in our maid Cora's room, at the top of the house, her face impossible to see in the darkness—or else on the sleeping car of a train, hurtling somewhere headlong off a trestle into a river thick and black as tar.*

I try to think about something calm: the new picture May's

painting of me reading, or the apples and honey Aleck has promised to send to us from the States, for Christmas.

Restless, I come to the memory of the summer when I was twenty-two—a good memory, this one is; maybe it will help me sleep. It's of the summer day Thomas came on a picnic with our cousins and us, to a lake. We were living then in our new house on Olive and Fifteenth, in Philadelphia, and we took the train to the country, and hired a carriage. Once we arrived at the lake, we spread out our baskets: eggs, a big jar of sassafras tea, apples, biscuits and honey. After we swam, we sat on the blanket and ate our fill. Thomas looked at me often, and after lunch we walked together up the slope. He brought a book out of his pocket— Emerson's essays, wasn't it?—and began to read. *Maybe this is what marriage will be like*, I thought: *to sit together on a hill, in Pennsylvania, looking at the edges of a lake, now blue, now greenish gray, and to read to each other, thinking of large things—of Nature and Spirit—as we sit wrapped, rapt, in a cloud, a net, of affection.*

My ceiling grows a dusky blue with dawn approaching. Of course I knew, even then, that marriage was more real, more difficult, than a romantic afternoon. I had seen all that Mother had been through,

26

with so many moves—once every year or two, often, difficult even to chart or remember—and her children's ill health, and her own fragile health, and Father's restlessness and impatience. But I found it hard to imagine my future in fuller detail, with Thomas half-leaning next to me, his hair still wet from his swim.

And when people see me now, what do they see? Certainly they can't know about a lake in Pennsylvania, or how a young man lay on his back, pulling me toward him, after reading for an hour while clouds scudded south.

viii.

Only the second day of modeling, and this picture is halfway done. I'm surprised by the urgency of my wish for this to continue: my sitting here, in this chair near the window, the lamp just over my shoulder, May painting, and the whole world at bay. Perhaps May feels something like this too, for she teases me now about my new profession.

"Be careful, Lyddy. You're such a good model, I'll find it difficult to let you go."

"Nonsense," I say, but I can't help smiling.

I asked May after breakfast this morning if I could pose with a book today, instead of the paper, and she agreed, as long as I read to her, and hold the newspaper again when she asks me. She added, "I'm not in the mood for Flaubert, though!" so I've left Emma Bovary at home, getting her thin boots muddy as she slips across the meadows to her shallow lover's *château*. I've brought my Wordsworth instead.

May asks for "Tintern Abbey," so I begin: "Five years have passed, five summers, and the length / Of five long winters." A splendid poem. It deepens as I grow older.

After I finish, May says, "You used to read that to me."

"Did I, May?"

"Yes, in Germany."

"I remember. I tutored you and Robbie, didn't I?"

"Yes," May says, but then she's quiet. She doesn't like to talk about that year.

When Robbie died, May was inconsolable. How old was she? Nine, ten. Ten years old, that must be right, because it was on May 24th, in '55, that he died; two days later, her birthday came and she was eleven. So I was almost eighteen.

She didn't touch the little cakes I'd bought. None of us seemed able to remember how to celebrate, even in the smallest way. I gave the cakes to the maid, and she thanked me for them.

It is at the funeral, in a cemetery in Darmstadt, where the minister speaks in

German, and cherry trees blossom up and down a slope, that May begins to cry. I try to embrace her, but she runs down the hill. I follow her to a cherry tree, covered in white blossoms. She stands near the tree, shaking and sobbing, and then she begins to hit the trunk with the side of her fist. "He was going to take lessons in drawing with me, when we got back to America. He said so. We were going to share a pony." She hits the tree with each sentence, pushing me away as I try to catch her arm and hold it. "I hate him for dying. He had no right to die."

I gaze at the page.

On the banks of this delightful stream / We stood together.

"I think it's almost done," May says now. "I think you'll be happy."

Bending toward the painting, I'm caught by its beauty. She's added a cloud, a light of pink, rose, around the edges, which surely hadn't been here, visible, and yet she's made something splendid with these colors. The woman reading seems suffused with rose. She holds a sheaf of papers, and what she reads seems to have dissolved into gray and pink and white.

"Alors?"

"It's lovely, May. Lovely."

"You like how the light's coming?"

"*Oui*."

"I think the colors have turned out well—the dress has been worrying me."

"The colors are splendid."

May turns to put away her oils.

"Maybe one more day," she says.

X.

May hurries to the studio this morning, and I walk as quickly as I can. As we reach the place Pigalle, and the outdoor tables at the Nouvelle Athènes, she grasps my arm and slows down.

"I'm like a race horse today, Lyddy, aren't I?"

I have to laugh. A race horse is just what she is, fine-tuned and restless, bolting for the finish. I glance across the busy *place* at Le Rat Mort, wondering whether Degas might be holding court today. Usually he waves to us, or rushes out to greet us. But Le Rat Mort shows no sign of him. I see only a couple of young men at a table, laughing, and a *vendeuse* gazing into the street, cradling a cup of coffee.

In her studio, May opens the curtains, and light swings into the room.

"Did you sleep well last night?" she asks.

"Quite well," I say, as confidently as I can.

"You feel quite well today?"

"Yes, May, quite well."

"I walked you here too fast, didn't I?"

"The walk was lovely."

"Have to keep you healthy, Lyddy. My best model."

"*Mais non*," I say, but I think to myself, with hesitant pride, yes, I am, I am quite a good model, and as soon as I think this, I chasten and mock myself, sending my thousand little bees to sting me, and sing their disdain: *How could you think*, the song always begins, and the thousand bees hum and mumble and murmur into my ear, adding new verses as they find new places to thrust their stingers in. *All you've done is sit here*, they hum, *and you're not even pretty, you're pale as a ghost and a bag of bones too*, and then the fiercer ones sing, *She's changed you into a figure of beauty, through oil and canvas, but how can you think she's pictured you as you really are?*

I'm used to these insects. I seem to own them, after all. They occupy a special place on my acre, complete with bee-boxes I myself seem to tend, in my veils and gloves. I'm their queen, as much as I'm the sorry object of their attacks. They fatten on my

31

clover and apple-blossoms and honeysuckle, and they practice their songs in the warm sun on my meadow. So I can't blame anyone but myself when they come to sting.

"I think Degas might come by today, Lyddy." May says this carefully, for I know she thinks I'm shy around him.

"Ah."

"He's eager to see the painting."

"Mm."

"He likes you very much. Only the other day he asked after you. He thinks so highly of you, Lyddy."

"Certainly he likes what he knows of me," I say. But I think to myself, maybe he's like my bees made visible? Can't May see how he could sting?

"He has been telling me he'd like to paint you one day, in fact."

"You must be joking, May." I almost slip out of my pose, to look at her.

"Why would I joke about that? You're a splendid model, he sees that." She adds, "He hopes to paint me, too."

Now I can't help breaking my pose to stare at May.

"You would pose for him?"

"Actually, I already have."

She has pulled her stubborn look, like a veil, over her face.

"Don't look so shocked, Lyddy. I don't show a bit of flesh, you know."

She's teasing me now; she pushes me to my limit, and then she smiles, her impish smile, polished to perfection since childhood, and I can't tell if she's making a fool of me or not.

Her face softens.

"*Ne t'en fais pas*. I've only modelled once or twice, Lyddy. Really, it's nothing to be worried about. He just needed someone to understand the pose, and I happened to be able to help him, when his other models couldn't."

"His other models?"

"You know what I mean."

"I'm not sure I do."

"Don't be so old-fashioned, Lyd. It's utterly *comme il faut*. Look at Berthe Morisot; she often sat for people, didn't she? She sat for Manet."

"Yes, and look at the women who are ruined by such men."

"Ruined! Lyddy, you sound as if you're in a novel."

"There's nothing fictional about it, May. It's ordinary life."

"Well." May looks at me soberly. "All I was trying to say was that Degas admires you."

33

"I am overwhelmed with gratitude."

As I move back into my pose, my head begins to hurt.

xi.

As the clock ticks the seconds, I find myself remembering the little girl who posed for May last spring, sitting in the blue armchair. I met her only once. She was shy and polite, the child of a friend of Degas.

How can I describe my uneasiness? It's just that, observing her, I saw freshly how a child has little real say about what happens. If my sister suggests she pose, so, and if Degas suggests she pose, so, and the child attempts to do what these grown-ups say, well, I suppose that's a child's life. And if the pose is indelicate, well, who is she to say so?

When the girl and her father left the studio that day, I attempted to bring this up with May, but she became furious and would hear none of it. *"Could you not move her legs closer together?"* I asked, in a gentle way. *"Oh, Lydia, how can you be so—American?!"* May exclaimed, her face growing red, just as it used to do when she was little. *"I am thinking simply of the child,"* I said. *"But what of the*

34

child, Lyd? The child is all right, she thinks nothing of the pose. Stop being so puritanical!" I felt my face grow hot when she said that, for I thought she might be right. I can't help having grown up in America, and I know May had to leave all that if she was to become something more than a lady portraitist or engraver. Yet I felt shame and anxiety for the child's situation. *"The pose is natural,"* May urged. *"She might loll in a chair like that at home. Who's to say a little girl should sit up straight, her hair brushed?"*

But May was deliberately misconstruing my meaning. To see those young legs, spread so widely apart, her arm bent back as if she were offering herself up as a small odalisque. May should have paid more attention. The child was not, after all, being painted by Degas.

Maybe my questions lingered in her, for she chose not to try another pose like that one. She even declined to have the little girl as a model again, although the child's father asked her many times. I've wondered, since then, if May herself began to feel apologetic toward the child, to have made such use of her. Not that she would ever say as much to me, or to anyone. She likes to feel she's right.

May confessed to me later that she'd allowed Degas to work on the background of that picture. I might have guessed, because of the strange cutting off of the chairs and windows by the picture's edges, and the dream-like proliferation of blue, flowered arm-chairs. Instead of one chair, three appear. A couch appears too, covered in the same blue material, not like any couch May owns, and all these pieces of furniture, placed at odd angles to each other, make a tense, unhappy family, having nothing to say to each other. May probably painted most of this, but I sense Degas' presence. He has a way of making a picture stirring and strange, like an unsettling dream.

She told me hesitantly. *"He helped me today."*

"Helped you?"

"He helped with the background."

"Did you ask him to?"

"I was surprised," she said, *"but I felt flattered."*

Flattered! This was May talking, fierce and independent May! "Well, do you like it better now?" I asked.

She looked at me then, a long, intricate look, and finally she said slowly, "I think he's added a certain brilliance to it, yes, and an unusual feeling."

"I know he's brilliant, May, and he paints unusual pictures. It's just that that painting is yours."

xii.

As we walk home this afternoon, arm in arm, I think about how I've created something with May, something that was not on earth before. As the crowds along the boulevard Rochechouart jostle us, I think I could fly home instead of walking.

Sitting in the lamplight, I try to read about Emma Bovary, whose life has swung terribly out of control, but all I can think about is May's picture. I miss something now, I'm not sure what. Maybe it's the posing I miss, or maybe it's the woman herself I'm missing, the one in the picture. I wish I could ask her a question, see her look at me. She has her own world now, a quiet and enchanted place, small and pleasant, composed of a few simple things: a chair, a newspaper, light. Sickness holds no place there. All is rose and white and cream, the gorgeous and simple here and now, the shimmering surface of things.

Yet at least she's safe. May has placed her in a world apart from the sting of bees and sickness, mortal life.

May has just asked me about my wishes. It's our old game. Each of us can say three. May's are easy; I could have spoken them for

37

her. "To become a famous and brilliant artist; to make lots of money; and to own a *château* to which all of us can retire in style." You don't have to tell the whole truth, in this game; half or less will do. I know some others of May's, I think, the ones she can't say, something about how love could still come to her, in some astonishing form, on the glint of a wing, cutting through air, and how those she loves—her sister, for instance, and in a different way, the terrible Degas—could hold the course.

She leans on my knees, looking up at me with a comical face. "And your wishes, Lyd?"

I think for a moment. "To become a famous and brilliant model," I say. ("Oh, I promise you that," May laughs.) "To live well, I mean mindfully. And"—I hesitate—"to have as much health as possible."

"Oh, make that a bigger wish, Lyddy," May says with sudden fierceness. "Say, 'To be utterly healthy, for fifty years at least.'"

"Touch wood, May," I say, and I think how health is only the beginning of my most ardent wish. *To live in that world you made,* I wish to say, *that creamy world of no difficulty, no blood. To know another's touch, and to have children of my own, like Aleck's, and a life like a shell curling in on itself, glistening and clean on the sand, rolled in salt water, rolled and rolled, spent and spending.*

May brings her face closer. "Model for me again."

38

Tea

I stand in an unmown meadow, green-gold, rimmed with dark green woods. I'm looking in the high grass—for what? A ring? A bracelet? I look at my hands and see I've forgotten my gloves

A raft of clouds, the line of trees darker

i.

This morning, the place d'Anvers looks covered in feathers, all shades of yellow and green. May and I walk up to the boulevard Rochechouart, through the cool air, and then the boulevard Clichy, past the cafés and boutiques. I'm wearing the dress I bought at Worth's before Easter, as deep pink as the inside of a conch shell. Whenever I'm about to pose for May now, I feel as if we've created a new holiday; I imagine marching along with banners flying.

In May's studio, I enter the pose she decided on yesterday. I hold a gold-rimmed cup and saucer in the purple-and-black striped satin armchair, near one of the long windows.

Looking through this window, holding this cup and saucer, I contemplate a slice of blue sky above the gray building opposite May's studio, a sheet of light clouds moving slowly. Near me, I know, hover white and grape hyacinths, although I can see them only out of the corner of my eye: a gift from Degas. I breathe in their scent.

May's skirt makes a rushing sound as she moves. I cherish the way the room fills with quiet, like a bowl filling with milk.

ii.

When Degas rings the bell, and a moment later bursts into the studio, our calm scatters. As I move out of my pose to greet him, I note his energy and elegance. His walking coat is the color of sand. He looks almost handsome.

"You're beginning a new one?" he asks in a moment, looking at the canvas.

"We began it yesterday," says May.

Degas studies the picture.

"The composition's all right."

"I'm glad you think so," May says wryly. She turns to me. "Shall we begin again, Lyd?"

"Certainly, May." I lower myself into the chair and pick up the cup and saucer. May touches my hand to bring the cup an inch closer to my face. "*C'est bien*. Just like that."

"The line of the arm—," Degas adds. "Well."

"Well?"

"*Et bien*, you might wish the angle—just there—of the elbow—to be sharper."

Looking out the window, I picture May standing next to Degas, her head cocked as she looks at the painting, and at me. He's quick to make suggestions. He can make jokes at her expense, too, as he does with other friends. Once he told her, in front of me, that something she'd just painted—an oil of a young woman in a theater—looked sweet and bland, like an English trifle. "One might like the first taste, but then, after a moment, one longs for something more—what?—nourishing." May retorted, "I think it's nourishing enough, thank you." She is not easily thrown off balance, although, in the privacy of our household, she sometimes lets me see how furious she is at him, or how distressed she feels by one of his remarks.

"If you were to move her arm just—so—you could make a more unusual effect."

"I like the angle of her arm. I think it works well."

"Oh, well, of course if you like it."

"I do."

iii.

Once May begins to paint, I hear Degas light his pipe, and I smell the pungent tobacco, as the pigeons whirr and the light in the studio grows brighter. I'm surprised he's staying so long today, and I'm not wholly happy. His presence changes things. For one thing, May becomes more self-conscious and alert. And I suppose I'm jealous of her attentions to him.

"Have you seen the reviews of our exhibition?" he asks May.

"Yes."

"Most of the critics are idiots."

"You come across rather well, though," May says. "Huysmans adores you."

Degas gives a short laugh. "Yes, and what did that elephant Ephrussi write? My subjects are 'bizarre,' the features of my dancers 'repulsive'?"

"He said more than that. He praised your drawing."

"Oh, well, then. I'm much in his debt."

"All of it was harder this year, with Monet at the Salon instead, and Renoir too."

"The world is full of self-serving people, attempting to puff

46

themselves up. What does art matter to them? If they want to parade in front of a stupid public, at the official bazaar, I have no need of them."

May isn't quite as irritated about friends like Renoir, but she too feels insulted, I know, by some of the reviewers of the *5ème* Impressionist exhibition this month. They find her colors too dark, her pictures not as interesting as the ones she presented last year, when she made such an astonishingly successful début. Henri Havard claims her originality has dimmed. Philippe Burty thinks her drawing misses "tonal strength," which is ridiculous, and he even blames her for—how did he put it?—"aspiring to the partially completed image." "He simply doesn't like what I'm trying to do," May says, throwing the newspaper on the couch. "Critics can be such fools."

I know she faults Degas, in part, for the haphazard air of this spring's exhibition. She worked all winter on prints to be published in the arts journal Degas envisioned, *Le Jour et la Nuit*, only to discover a few weeks ago, right before the exhibition was to open, that Degas felt his own prints were not ready. And, because he was not ready, the whole journal was abandoned. She had only eight oil paintings ready for the show; so much of her effort had gone into her printmaking.

May felt angry with Degas, just as Pissarro and the others did. Yet she has not stayed angry. "After all, I could have painted more," she says. "I'll have to do more this year, that's all there is to it. I'll have the critics on their knees next spring."

As a girl, of course, she proved she could hold herself the equal of anyone, including Father, who has never been one to hold back his thoughts. He tried to prevent her from doing so many things: taking art classes in Philadelphia, studying and travelling on her own in Europe, living in Paris. He couldn't understand why she wouldn't simply stay in Philadelphia and marry. "You could keep painting, May. We do have some culture in America, you know."

She holds her own with Degas too. Something teasing and fierce is in their friendship. Although she acknowledges that his wit can be too caustic, she relishes it sometimes, and she certainly admires his intelligence and his devotion to art. All year, she has seen him almost daily, making use of his printing press, experimenting with various methods, brushing shoulders with him at his studio or hers, at museums or dealers, and of course at our apartment too. She even began to pose for him more often in the winter (*and May Alcott died just after Christmas*, the memory glancing into my mind like a bird, and flying off again, *her face pale, the infection from childbirth ravaging her*).

May still poses for Degas, probably more than I know. Of course, she's not like his other models. I've often been with her in his studio as she poses, looking into a mirror, trying on a hat, sitting with her folded umbrella. These pictures bear almost no resemblance to the others I know he's painting now, of dancers, their arms and shoulders bare, their legs muscular in tights. Awkward these figures are, ugly sometimes. He shows them in harsh light, from unflattering angles, laboring to raise their legs, or resting, exhausted from their labor.

I've heard rumors about other pictures he's working on, of subjects too risqué for public view. I wonder if May has seen them.

Looking out the window, for all the world like someone at a party, I hold a pretty, empty cup and gaze at the ribbon of blue sky. I watch quick brush strokes of birds, rich gray against blue, and listen to the subtle tones in my sister's conversation with Degas, the shadings, the slow move off into another color. *How close to May does he stand?* I wonder. *How do they look at each other?*

"You'll both come to my *soirée* this Saturday, I hope?"

"Of course we will, won't we, Lyd?"

"I hope so."

49

To brush shoulders with his and May's friends—Renoir, Caillebotte, Pissarro, and others—to feel alive in that bright, crowded space, makes a heady kind of joy. If the ticket of entrance is the risk of the host's acid wit, well then, I suppose I too am willing to pay the price.

"And I am hoping you'll sit for me again one day, Mademoiselle Cassatt."

"I'm honored," I say, holding my pose. This is at least a partial truth. The pleasure I felt, in modeling for him last January with May, surprised me. In his studio, he posed me sitting down, holding a guidebook. The idea, he explained, was that we were in the Louvre, possibly the Etruscan gallery, two visitors, one standing, one sitting.

How can I describe the sensation of being looked at by this man? His look felt, at moments, like a storm on a coast, stirring the trees to wildness, shifting the dunes. I hadn't felt prepared.

The thickness in the air of May's studio becomes palpable. I imagine opening my mouth to eat it like bread.

"I'm sorry, May. Did you say something?"

"Lyddy! I thought you were listening! We were just talking

about this summer. I'm encouraging Monsieur Degas to come out to the country to visit us, when we rent our house in Marly."

"Ah. Of course. That will be lovely."

"You must enjoy the country, Mademoiselle Cassatt."

"*Oui*. It can be so hot in Paris in the summer."

"Our nephews and nieces will be visiting," May adds. "Our brother Aleck will be coming over from the States with his wife and four children. My sister is eager to begin spoiling them again."

"I think we spoil them equally." I smile, just to think of them. I think of Gard too, on his own now in Philadelphia, a bachelor still. I long to see him. Outside the window, high up, the white-fleeced clouds have begun to come apart, into feathered fragments.

"And will you work there?" Degas speaks to May, his voice gravelly and low.

"I'll do what I can. I can paint outdoors, in good weather."

"Yes. I'd like to see what you do."

"You'll come and see."

"*Oui*. I'll come and see."

"Lyddy seconds my invitation."

"*Bien sûr*, of course I do."

The light has moved from my chair to the floor beside me, and soon, I know, it will become something diffuse, not pouring in these bands onto the parquet. It will become, more, a thought, an idea of light.

iv.

"Ready for a rest, Lyd?"

As I move out of my pose, I see my sister standing by her easel, looking exhilarated and tired. Degas lounges in the armchair nearest May, his eyes heavy-lidded, like a lizard's in the sun. He rises slowly to his feet, as I rise.

Looking at the painting, I see a woman, clothed in pink and white, the white (my dress's lace) making a brilliant cloud around her neck, and again at the opening of her sleeve, with a tumult of color (the hyacinths) around her head. I bend closer to the woman's face, her chin half-hidden in the whiteness, her forehead in the swirls of golden-red, her eyes, touched with quick strokes of blue, looking elsewhere, her mouth half-smiling, holding in her thoughts.

Look at me, I long to say to her. *Tell me, what are you thinking, as you*

The Cup of Tea, The Metropolitan Museum of Art, from the Collection of James Stillman, Gift of Dr. Ernest G. Stillman, 1922. (22.16.17) Photograph © 1998 The Metropolitan Museum of Art.

begin to bring this gold-rimmed cup to your mouth? Absurd, I know, this longing.

"Alors?" May looks at me, questioning.

"It's beautiful, May."

"Do you really like it?"

"Of course I do. The color is beautiful."

Can't you think of another word? I wonder. May is waiting for something more. I feel unable to tell her all my thoughts: how I yearn to be this woman, to be composed of this swirling, lovely world, not Lydia, not myself, feeling exhausted and cold suddenly, my head hurting, as Degas looks over our shoulders.

"Very pretty," he says.

"Pretty! Don't insult me."

He throws her a teasing, dark smile. "Oh, well, you know it's very good," he says. "You have an enviable sense of line. A woman shouldn't be allowed to have such a sense of line." He adds, "Of course, you're lucky in your model."

"The model has little to do with it," I say.

"Au contraire. A model has an immense amount to do with it." He looks at me with amusement.

"Of course she does. Lyddy, you're absurdly modest." She

points to her canvas. "I'm going to do more with the dress and the background, and a bit more with the face. I can't make you pose any longer today. And the light's changed."

"I can come tomorrow," I say, although my head is beginning to ache in earnest. My illness rushes back to me, sometimes, like this.

"Lyddy." I feel May's hand in mine. I have bent over, and someone has lowered me into a chair.

"I'm all right, May."

I feel her hand on my forehead, and then her fingers under my chin, untying my bonnet.

"Some water for her, please, Edgar."

"Of course."

Soon a cup is held to my lips, but I shake my head.

"I'll be all right."

And then I am inside my illness again. All that happens means nothing to me— the long walk out of May's studio to the street, the cab ride home. I am half-aware that I have ceased to care what anyone thinks of me, even Degas, who rides with us in the cab, looking strangely shaken.

Days can be passed this way, lying in bed, shrouded in the duvet I love when I am well, and that now seems to rub and hurt, to be all wrong, just as the world is wrong in each detail. Sounds that could give pleasure to someone healthy seem to prick me until I'm a bloody mess: Lise placing the washing bowl on my table, Mother's voice calling to May, the clattering of silver and plates, Batty's yips, and, muffled but upsetting, the sounds of avenue Trudaine.

I am not fit for this life. I hold still, hoping the illness will decide to go away, leaving me empty and picked clean, a thin replica of myself, but at peace and alive, like small bird bones on a cliff, that miraculously begin to sing.

I call to Lise, or to May if she's home. My mouth opens and my stomach pitches and heaves. Mother comes too slowly, and I can't bear to ask her to clean up my messes. Lise is immature, and dislikes illness; she wrinkles her nose and holds her breath, sighing and making a show of taking the basin away. May's better, because she has courage, and backbone, but she cannot disguise her distress at my condition.

Why is it that I feel at fault for this sickness? Surely I am not at fault. In the midst of my collapse, I feel fury at my family, the way they tiptoe around me and look at me with hushed faces, as if I've already died; and yet, at the same time, they seem impatient with me. *Be healthy or go, choose one or the other,* I imagine them thinking, *we can't bear to accompany you further into this illness.*

vi.

May has become restless. She's lost days, nursing me. Often she has even had to bathe me, for I've been too ill to bathe myself. I worry that she's disgusted with my body, pale and ungainly, my breasts heavy, too intimate for a sister's hand, the washcloth moving here and there, *my body a place I wish I could leave, like walking out of our garden at Hardwicke, and slipping through the gate into the meadow.*

Yet I love to have May near. She's been painting and working, on prints, I think, each morning (*and who does she see?*), but she comes home midday now, instead of continuing. Sometimes she reads to me, and sometimes, when I'm feeling very sick, she sits on my bed and holds my hands. When we're both lucky, her presence makes me feel calm, and allows sleep to come.

I cherish time with May. But I do not wish to pay this price for her presence.

vii.

I wake this morning to see May in the chair next to my bed. Someone has opened my curtains, and the sun spills onto the far wall, and onto my embroidery frame. May looks tired and determined, her face framed by her crimson bonnet and royal blue silk scarf. She's wearing a light gray coat. *If I could paint you now,* I think, *this is how I'd see you, tired and luminous, your face half in shadow, the light around you changing the air to cream.* She begins to pull on her beige gloves, and to work at the pearl buttons. She glances at me appraisingly.

"You look better."

"Well, that's a blessing."

"You've worried me."

"I worry myself."

I watch her button the last button and smooth her coat. For a moment, I think of my body as a kind of landscape, across which

I can travel, checking the trees and roads, seeing whether the bridges have held during the tumult of this week. It feels like a luxury simply to have a thought.

In the midst of this calm, I remember the painting. How must it look, in the light of May's studio?

"What day is it today?" I could ask, what season? What year?

"Monday."

I try to calculate how long I've been sick. May seems to guess my thoughts.

"You've been in bed for five days."

"Ah. I'm sorry about the painting, May."

"The painting's almost done. It can wait until you're well."

I study her face. She looks pale, and the circles under her eyes look deeper. She has been up with me many times this week, in the middle of the night. *And am I at fault, then?*

"What will you do today?"

"Oh." May looks careless. "I have lots to do."

"You have another model?"

May looks at me quickly.

"I can always find someone." She gazes at me for a minute. "I won't be able to find anyone like you, Lyd."

"Nonsense."

"You know it's true."

She looks out the window.

As she leaves my room, I say, "*Courage*, May."

viii.

Being ill, one has lots of time to think. Too much time. One's whole life comes to the bedside, to pay a visit, welcome or unwelcome. At some moments, the visitor seems to be some monstrous and misshapen figure, crouched on my chest, refusing to leave and presenting picture after picture of all that I remember. I find myself sifting through my insults to others, to May when she was little, to Aleck, to Gard, and to Robbie, before he died. I remember too my sense of bereavement, waving to Aleck from the ship as it embarks from New York. He grows smaller, to the size of a dab of paint, and I feel that in that figure, almost invisible now, resides my own childhood. *Will you marry Thomas? he asked, as we sat on the kitchen steps together one night. I was twenty-three. Yes. Yes, I will.* And, strangely, May Alcott threads through these memories, unbidden. I picture her as she looked when I last saw her, her ill face framed by the white pillow, her eyes closed. For three weeks last December she lay in a coma, in her house in Meudon.

Such thoughts become part of my illness, entwining with my nausea and my headache—a whole ocean pounding in my head. Can memories hurt? Then these hurt. I feel at moments as if I'm in an ongoing dream of sickness and grief, yearning to wake up into a new day.

In the midst of my illness, I discover an urgent wish to pose again. As I lie here, absurdly weak, I long to enter May's studio, to hold the cup and saucer again, or a book, or anything.

To model for someone is always a surprise; you never know what they'll make of you. After I posed for Degas, last winter, he completed various pictures using his original sketch—etchings, pastels, some placing us in the Etruscan gallery, one in another room of the Louvre. Looking at them, I saw, with painful lucidity, how he might see me—I mean, how he might actually see me, outside of the picture. The way he had posed both of us had been comical, really. We looked like two tourists braving the Louvre. I sat to the side, the guidebook held up to my face, covering my chin, while May stood, insouciant, attractive, her curved back to the viewer, her umbrella at a sharp angle to the floor, appearing far more interested in her own elegance than in the incomprehensible and stirring art she faced.

Of course, May and I couldn't know how we would look, especially once Degas added the image of the Etruscan gallery. In the etching, May contemplated and I peeked at a splendid sarcophagus of a half-naked husband and wife leaning and looking out of a glass case, as if to gaze back at us. When he showed me this version of the picture, I felt offended, to see this timid woman, hiding behind a book, barely able to look at the sumptuous couple, lounging in their eternal bed. I know it's silly to feel offended by the way someone portrays me—after all, this was not meant to be a portrait—but I felt offended nonetheless. May just praised the etching for its sense of composition and line, and she laughed, unbothered, at the wit of it.

I wish I could have responded with May's self-confidence, with her love of the satire in Degas' art. She's right to respond this way. But all I could think was, *Of course. Of course this is how he must see me.* I found myself arguing with him in my imagination, a fruitless exercise, telling him, *But you're wrong, I'm not such a timid soul. Whatever I look at, I look at wholeheartedly and with as clear an eye as even you can turn on the world.*

ix.

When Mother comes into my room, I welcome her presence as a relief and a distraction from such thoughts. In the chair next to my bed, she sits quite naturally in the present, here in our apartment, knitting, reading the newspaper, writing letters to friends in America, and to Aleck and Gard. She enjoys my company, and makes few inquiries into my inner state. I join her on the surface, in this here and now, leaving the welter of my emotions out of the picture. As I talk to her, I fold up most of my nettling memories, wrap them in paper, and tuck them into drawers, as Cora and the other maids used to do with our clothes when one season turned into another, in each house we occupied. I look around the room, and out the window, aware of the light, the color of the sky.

"I'm writing to Aleck," Mother says, adjusting her specs. "I'm asking him whether your youngest brother Gardner has any thought of marriage in his frivolous soul." Her silver hair is in a *chignon* under her cap. Her rings flash small bits of color.

I embrace the thought of handsome Gard, and of Aleck's brood, Eddie and Sister and Robbie and Elsie. I remember how I held Elsie, the youngest, on the day of her birth in Philadelphia. Such a tight little bundle of flesh, her forehead silk. I put my hand in the basin of warm water, to wash the baby, *the bloody sheets, Lois a bloated and exhausted ghost of herself. Will she live? I wondered, frightened.*

"Elsie must be so big now."

"Oh, yes. Lois says she's a handful." Mother looks at me with a wry smile.

"The children will love the country."

Mother nods. "May will have to take them on lots of expeditions."

"She's been talking about showing them Versailles too."

"Versailles would be splendid. They can see the fireworks."

"Maybe May will paint the children."

"*If* they can sit still," says Mother. "You know May has no patience for wriggling."

Children are excellent medicine.

X.

I am awoken, mid-afternoon, out of a troubled sleep by May sitting on my bed. She's breathless from her walk up the five flights to our apartment. My dream disperses (*a soldier, his face blasted, my own hands red with blood*).

I rub my eyes and look at May, as she unbuttons her gloves, pulling at the buttons in her impatience.

"I've found a new model, Lyd. Actually, two."

"I'm glad," I say, although I catch another feeling before it tries to slip away: jealousy, is it?

"One of them is quite young."

"*Ah bon?*" My jealousy bites more sharply.

"Yes. And quite restless."

"Restless?"

"Wriggly."

I stare at May, and she laughs. "*En effet*, it's hard to sit still when you're under a year old."

"Ah." I'm aware of my relief. "You've found a child?"

"Our landlady's great-nephew. Her niece is visiting, from Dieppes."

"How did you ask them to model? You've asked the child's mother, too?"

"Yes." May looks very satisfied with herself. "I met them just outside Madame Phillippe's apartment. The baby lay asleep in his carriage. He has golden hair, Lyd, like a cherub, a Tiepolo cherub."

"I'd love to see him." My bedroom feels small suddenly, even smaller than usual, as confining as a hatbox.

"I'm sure you'll have a chance to see him. They're staying for a week with Madame Phillippe."

"Bring them up for tea, May."

"If you feel well enough."

"I'll feel well enough. In a day or two. I'm sure the baby would love Batty."

"I'm not sure Batty would love *him*. But I'll try to bring them up anyway."

This afternoon, May has brought a picture home, a pastel. Two figures, a woman and a baby, embrace, the child's arm tight around her neck. I'm amazed by the way she's shown only the delicate sides of their heads; you can't see their faces at all. The mother bends in, to kiss the baby, and all one can see is the line of the mother's cheek and part of her brow, the soft cheek of the baby. How astonishing, to place the kiss just out of our vision. It's as if May's saying, *this is something you can only imagine, for these figures have no need of you. Your look can only go so far.*

"How did you do this, May?"

"I had to get it down quickly, especially the shapes, and this line." She traces the soft "V" of the mother's cheek, cradled between the baby's small arm and head.

"*Mais*, how did you think of this pose?"

"I wished for two figures, so close they seem to mesh. I wanted the faces to be a mystery."

"I can almost feel the baby's cheek."

May is quiet for a moment. Then she adds, "I wished to create the sense of a moment of utter closeness. It's quick and spontaneous, but, in the painting, it holds, it stays."

I think of Degas' dancers, exhausted, hard at work, isolated from each other and from the dance master, or from the men who linger in hallways off-stage. Sometimes you see only legs, the torso cut off by the painting's frame, and often you find yourself in an odd relationship to his figures: spying on them, or looking down at them. The space between them is fraught, nervous. I can't remember seeing a picture of Degas' in which two figures embrace, right at the center, so close you could touch them, and I certainly can't imagine him painting a subject like this, so fresh and joyous, so spontaneous: a mother and a baby, utterly in love. The strength of the lines, the boldness of the colors and the design, is pure Mary Cassatt.

"I know of no one else who could have created this, May."

She looks at me, flushed, triumphant. "I know."

I look again at the pastel: the rich blue color of the armchair, the deep green of the woman's dress, the gold and white of the child's hair and chemise, the auburn of the mother's hair, the restless greens and reds of the wallpaper pattern behind them, the mysterious and gorgeous shadow, in red, between the mother's face and the baby's. The whole composition centers there, in that red shadow, in that ardent and unseen kiss.

I carry them inside me now, those two figures, holding each other in a fierce embrace. *Arm and arm, cheek and cheek, in a swirl of color and brightness. Two figures bending in to each other.*

xii.

Today I am well enough to be brought into the parlor, in honor of Isabelle's and Michi's visit. May has just finished her oil of them; I hope to see it soon. May says it's a bathing picture, in a *déshabillé*. She borrowed one of my white morning dresses, and the Delft washing bowl from my room. "You'll like this one, Lyddy," she says.

Michi in the flesh holds a chocolate éclair as he sits, happy as a drunken sailor, on Isabelle's knee. He's dressed in a Tartan frock with a white pinafore, and his little brown shoes seem to be conducting a frenzied, happy orchestra. Isabelle has a gentle manner. She listens politely to May and to Mother and Father, as they describe our nieces and nephews in America. I present Michi with a gift of little wool socks, and May gives him a new toy-book by Kate Greenaway.

"You'll be leaving for Dieppes soon?" Mother asks, in French, offering Isabelle sliced melon.

"*Merci bien, madame. Oui*, we leave tomorrow morning."

"Will you be coming back to Paris in the coming year, *madame?*" Father asks.

Isabelle smiles. "*Je l'espère, monsieur*. Only, our family may be growing larger this year, and you know, it becomes more difficult to travel."

Michi grabs a *marron confit* from Isabelle's plate, and offers it to Father. Father accepts with good humor. Batty sits on the rug near Isabelle, wagging his tail and looking up at Michi, hopeful that a *marron* or an *éclair* might fall to the floor.

Later, after the small company manages to bundle themselves out the door, all of us seem to feel momentarily bereft. Mother sighs and Father picks up *Le Temps* half-heartedly, throwing himself into his armchair. May walks up and down a few times, glancing into the mirror over the fireplace, and then gazing out the window on the south side of the parlor, her forehead on the glass: from that window, I know, she sees all of Paris. I open my book—*Sonnets from the Portuguese*, my old copy, dog-eared—and try to read, but all I can think of is Michi's plumpness and cheerfulness. I wish May had made dozens of pictures of him, so we could imagine him here.

May comes to sit on the ottoman near me.

"She was a good model, wasn't she?" I ask.

"*Oui.*"

"And the baby too."

"The baby too."

"You'll have the children to paint this summer," I remind her.

"*Oui.* You're right, Lyd."

"You're very good at painting children, you know, May."

"Do you think so?" May looks younger for a moment. She searches my face.

"I do. I most certainly do. You're brilliant at it."

"I was surprised myself, how well the pictures came out."

I glance at my book.

The face of all the world is changed, I think, / Since first I heard the footsteps of thy soul.

"The good thing is, May, you'll always be able to find wonderful models, in children."

May's face is hard to interpret. "Yes, Lyddy, that's true."

xiii.

It's like a gift, the oil painting, when May shows it to me: a calm
moment, a mother squeezing a cloth in a blue and white basin,
her hand large and strong, her other hand holding a sleepy
child, legs akimbo, eyes half-open, gazing at her, her face bent to
gaze back, her forehead touched with light, her morning dress a
white landscape on which he rests, becalmed, idle, in this
moment before bathing, so clear, so still, that it remains cut out
of time. Always the hand hovers, poised, in the water of the
basin, always the mother bends to her baby, always the baby
bends toward her. Outside the room, the world moves on, with
its ships and trains, its republics, its foreign colonies, its industry,
its injustice, its wars, its terror. The world becomes merely a
thought about something other than this quietness, this room,
this careful love.

*Elsewhere now, the bloody sheets, the baby's cry, the exhausted face, cherry
trees on a hillside, dirt tossed onto a box of wood, agony and then absence.*

I'm better now, much better. Mother still thinks she and May should take me to one of the spas, perhaps to Pau, although Father blusters about needing them to stay with him in Paris, "and we've already sent the money for the house in Marly, May, I doubt we can get that back." I agree with him, although for different reasons. The thought of having to brush shoulders with hordes of English tourists, taking the water, is enough to make me ill again. And if I were in Pau for two months, I would miss half of Aleck's visit. I will have better food, and more peace and quiet, in the country with my family than I would at the baths.

On my second good day, May helps me into the deep pink dress again, and waits as I descend the stairs from our apartment one at a time. Mathieu brings our carriage to the front of the building, and we ride in style along avenue Trudaine to the rue des Martyrs, and up to the boulevard Clichy. The district looks bright this morning, awash with late spring. The air feels softer, and, as I step carefully out of the carriage, holding May's hand, a wave of satin holds me up, helps me move more lightly.

After the morning's brightness, May's studio looks at first a dusky blue, and I shiver. As May opens the curtains, and then the windows, light changes the color of the floors to a shiny wheat, touching the corner of the marble mantelpiece and turning it from dark gray to silvery blue. Even the farthest corners grow lighter, and this other world emerges again: the mahogany tea table, the plump armchairs, the folded throws and cloths, the cups and saucers, the Japanese vases, the Turkish rugs, the mirror over the mantel. The gold hands of the clock say a quarter to ten.

I almost laugh. What a feat! By some miracle, or God's grace, or astonishing luck, here I am again, in this room, with my sister, on a spring morning in Paris, about to engage in the creation of a concoction, a vision, made of oil paints on canvas.

And here she is still, the woman in the picture, holding her cup and saucer, about to drink her tea, a smile on her face, for all the world as if she is at a party, her dress a rich pink, the lace around her neck a spray of white water.

"Of course the hyacinths have gone," May says, as I sit in the purple chair. I look around. Of course. The high green table too is gone.

"Could you find more hyacinths, May?"

"I'm not sure. But it's all right. I like what I have of them."

She moves my chin, and touches my right hand.

"*C'est bien*. Hold that."

And I do. I hold the pose, in joyful relief that I am here to hold it. I welcome even the ache in my arms, the tingling in my fingers, the urge to move.

Illness has this edge of grace. If the illness lifts, even for a few days, and one can enter the world again, all things shine with clarity and value. This cup, so light, becomes a miracle. And how much more a miracle that my sister looks at this cup, and at me, and touches a brush to mounds of oil on her palette, and makes a design that places me at the center of her creation. I am indeed comforted.

The Garden

and then I see May, and she's small, only two or so, running through the meadow, and I catch her up and hold her. She's hot. She cries, "Baby." "There's no baby here," I say, running my fingers through her hair, and

Marly-le-Roi, septembre, 1880

i.

The garden hums. A piercing blue sky, and a hot sun, mid-morning. My gloves warm, as I hold my crochet hook and the blue thread.

"Lyddy. Could you hold your hands still for a while? I'm trying to get them."

I hold my hands still. I gaze at my gloves and the hook until my eyes begin to water. Keeping my head in the pose, slightly bent, I look up and to the side for a moment to see May. The lace of my white bonnet appears like an umbrella, held at a slant over her. Her white blouse looks damp, with a blue oil stain on the front. She frowns as she studies my hands. She is standing, dabbing her brush on the palette. I blink a few times, and look at my crochet hook, wishing I could make my next stitch.

"I'm in great danger of making your fingers look like sausages." May sounds annoyed with herself.

"Maybe they do look like sausages."

I glance at May's face again to see her smile, and then I gaze at my gloves, the color of tea with milk. I added the fine red stitching, in three lines, on the back of each one.

Soon my arms begin to hurt, and my fingers do feel bunched up, swollen, but my gloves and the day still shine.

"What are you making, Lyddy?"

"A shawl for Elsie's doll."

"Corabella?"

"Yes. Corabella." I picture Corabella's surprised blue eyes in her porcelain face, her bird's nest of flaxen hair, her porcelain legs and arms, with one of the toes chipped. One hand too has been broken, and Elsie insists on a new bandage every few days.

"Poor Corabella leads a difficult life," May observes.

"She is devoted to Elsie, however."

"*Oui*. Elsie is most certainly the sun and moon of Corabella's world."

This is an island, composed of May and me, her brush and my gloves, my aching and her gaze. On her canvas, I become a healthy woman in blue and white. Sun and brush heal me, brush and sun, and French birds in a French garden.

Astonishing, how this place—this garden, our rented house, the village—thrives, a short train ride from Paris. The Seine is a ribbon, waving through this countryside, out of the city. If I could, I would walk from Marly to Port Marly, or even to the bridge in Bougival, to see the river, as May has done sometimes with Berthe Morisot, who summers nearby. The air is good here. I've suggested to my family that we could live in Marly all year round, or in Louveciennes, but May feels too isolated in the country. She loves the rush of Paris, the closeness to galleries and to her friends. Degas lives only a quick walk from our apartment there. She has become restless, after three months in this village.

I find myself picturing a little house, all my own, full of books, here in Marly, snow on my pillowcase of a lawn, a small garden of flowers I like best, an armchair by a window.

Quick, light steps on the walk. At first I think it's Elsie, until I remember she's on the boat to America; Aleck and Lois sailed home with all of the children a week ago.

"*Bonjour, mesdemoiselles, où est Batty?*" Vivi hops in front of me, in a blue linen dress and a white pinafore. Her older sister must have come to help Mother with the mending.

"*Pourquoi?* Do you wish to play with him?" May asks in French.

"Oui, mademoiselle."

"Run into the house and find him, and tell Madame Cassatt that I gave you permission."

"Merci bien, mademoiselle." The child curtsies and runs to the house. Soon I hear Batty's sharp bark, like a small gold hammer—*tin, tin, tin!*—and the girl's high voice, as she tells him how they will go to the stream, and possibly see a fish or a frog.

Only a week ago Vivi played with Sister and Elsie near the roses, carting Corabella and Sister's doll Joanna in the wheelbarrow. Elsie brought me two handfuls of rose petals one day and asked if I could make something out of them for Corabella. "Petals are too delicate for needle and thread," I said, "and besides, they'll fade soon, and dry up." "Could you try anyway?" she asked. "Corabella likes roses, and she needs a new shawl too." So I shall surprise patient Corabella with this blue, lacy shawl. It will be getting colder in Pennsylvania soon.

I miss the children immensely. I almost say this to May, but I know she knows this. She misses them too, although of course she has her painting, and her friends. My longing for them is a hunger I cannot satisfy. I had not known I could love them this much.

Batty's bark is more distant. I think of Elsie, chasing Batty. She would squeal when she caught him, and he would wiggle and snap at her. If I were to paint Elsie, this is the picture that would first come to me. I could not comprehend her love of the difficult—of the very thing that spurned her.

"Elsie adores Batty," I say.

"Oh yes, and poor Batty is terrified of Elsie."

"Batty is terrified of nothing."

May laughs. "You know very well he's terrified of everything. That's why he barks so much."

I hesitate. "Like the person who gave him to you?"

May laughs. "*C'est vrai*, Degas certainly can bark." In a moment, she adds, "I think it's possible he can be frightened of his own bark. That is, on his good days. He can be kind, Lyddy, *n'est-ce pas?*"

"Certainly, he can be kind. He was kind to the children this summer," I say.

"Remember how he brought them *bonbons?*"

"*Oui*, he brought *bonbons*." I smile. "Is this our new litany, May? Shall we call it 'In Praise of Degas'?"

"I know he isn't a saint."

"A saint? No. I don't expect anyone of my acquaintance to be a saint."

"Well, what about you, Lyd? Surely you're a saint, if anyone is."

"Mais non, May." I look at her. "People always think a woman saintly if she's simply single, and not entirely self-centered."

"Et bien, I'm not entirely self-centered," May says, "and I'm single, and no one thinks of me as a saint."

I gaze at my gloves again, and the blue thread. *"C'est vrai.* Saintliness isn't the first word that comes to mind in describing you, May. Maybe it's because you have such ambition. I suppose a saint's only ambition should be to serve God."

"And your ambition, Lyddy? What do you desire in the world?"

"Me? I don't suppose my desires are much different from any other woman's."

May holds her brush in the air. She looks as if she wishes to say something, but then she looks at her canvas.

"I would have married, for instance, if I could have," I add. "Although I wouldn't call that my ambition."

"Would you have wished to marry, Lyddy?"

"Of course. If I could have married someone I loved."

I glance at May. She's looking expectantly at me.

"But, I remember, that year I began studying art in Philadelphia, someone asked you, *non?*"

"Who?" I look at her, puzzled, thinking of Thomas Houghton (*in the garden, at dusk, behind our West Chester house, his face glimmering in the*

84

Lydia Crocheting in the Garden, The Metropolitan Museum of Art, Gift of Mrs. Gardner Cassatt, 1965. (65.184) Photograph © 1993 The Metropolitan Museum of Art.

dark. *"Lyddy!" I heard someone calling, from inside the house. I looked at him, and the air between us seemed sweet and slow. "Lyddy!")*

"The Harvard student, with the curly hair. You must remember, Lyddy, he fawned over you for months."

"Oh." I laugh. "You mean Joshua Winthrop."

"He was studying to be a minister."

"Yes. Oh, heavens, no, I could never have married him. Poor old Joshua, with the crooked teeth and the earnest smile. His idea of courtship was to offer me wise quotations."

"And your idea of courtship?"

"Oh, May."

"You brought up the subject, Lyddy. I was seven years younger, you know, and full of curiosity about you. You were so private. You never let me in on anything."

"I doubt there was much to let you in on."

"Oh, I don't know, Lyd. I would guess the opposite."

"Stop!"

"And what about that other young man, what was his name? The one from Virginia, who rode so well? He was handsome, I remember."

"You must be an elephant, May, you don't forget anything! You mean William, William Dabney."

"Yes. One of Aleck's friends. You sat in the parlor with him one night."

"Oh, yes, with my whole family walking in and out, not to mention old Nora, limping with her hind leg, and putting her nose into his lap!" *Quiet, William was, and shy, although when I looked up from something I was doing—currying a horse, weeding, pulling on my old boots—I'd see him looking at me.* "He was much too shy, May. It would have taken him five years to start a real conversation. And anyway, I was thinking of another by then."

"Was that Thomas?"

I am surprised at the way my throat feels thick, suddenly. I cannot speak. The blue thread wavers in front of my eyes.

"I remember one summer," May adds. "Everywhere I turned, there you were with him."

"Yes." *his hand touching my arm, my shoulder, his voice murmuring. "Lyddy."*

"Et?"

"Et?"

"What happened?"

I shrug. "It was so long ago, May. I'm not sure I can even remember what happened." *the air sweet and slow, threads thrown out between us making a fine mesh, pulling us in*

"You were engaged, weren't you?"

"Engaged. *Oui.*" *Slipping into the garden one night, in West Chester, after a day of swimming, we embraced for the first time, fiercely, hungrily, in the humid summer air, the rich, fragrant grass, with the sound of our dog Nora barking from the front lawn, children's voices calling to us, "Lyddy! Thomas!"*

My fingers feel numb, and the back of my neck aches. I sense the first signs of nausea, but I will it to hold off. How can I be no longer the young woman in the garden, wishing to be seen, and touched, my desire meshed with another's?

On that August day, Degas hovered behind May's chair as she sketched Elsie. His hand touched the nape of May's neck. He caressed her neck for a moment, and she leaned into him.

I listen to old Josephe rolling the wheelbarrow. The asters have come into bloom now. He's been weeding this morning, pulling out the straggling annuals, clipping the long pointed leaves of the irises. I have asked him if I may help plant the bulbs, and he's agreed.

I've told May that I wish to start a little garden on our balcony this spring, in Paris, because I won't be able to wait until summer.

"Oh, Lyddy," she says, "summer will come again before you know it."

"Lyddy?"

    "*Oui?*"

    "What are you thinking?"

    "Oh, I was just thinking about gardening."

    "Gardening?"

    "It's amazing, how gardens help you understand each season."

    "Except for winter, I suppose, when snow covers everything."

    "Remember the snowdrops, by the front steps of Hardwicke, May, how they pushed up through the snow?"

It's like a dream I had, that August afternoon, here in Marly. As I walked in the garden, after lunch, I came upon something I could not at first comprehend. Two figures, one in dark trousers, a white shirt, blue suspenders, one in a yellow dress, embracing. The world bent closer, and slowed: the allée, the summer leaves, the roses climbing the arbor.

ii.

May's moving quickly now, brush to palette to canvas, and I resist the urge to move. To pose, after all, is to agree to a form of enchantment.

I hear Batty's bark, muffled through the trees and growing louder. Soon I hear Vivi running along the *allée*, and Batty scrabbling and barking—*tin, tin, tin!*

"You may rest, Lyddy."

I move slowly out of my pose, to see Vivi rushing up, flushed and winded. May bends to pick up her little dog.

"*Alors, monsieur,*" she says, stroking his small head as he pants, "what adventures did you have with Vivi?"

Batty's eyes glitter as he licks her hands.

"He barked at a squirrel, *mademoiselle*, and almost fell into the stream."

May laughs. "Poor old Batty!"

She stretches. "Shall I release you, Lyddy? It's almost one. Father will be anxious to begin lunch, and your sister will be waiting for you, Vivi."

I stand up, trying not to wince at the pain in my back.

"When will Elsie come back to Marly, *mademoiselle?*" Vivi asks, taking my hand.

"Oh, soon. In a year, maybe," I say.

"A year! I'll be so much older then. Do you think she'll know who I am?"

"*Bien sûr.* She'll know you right away."

My back hurts, but I take a breath and feel Vivi's hand in mine, her fingers fine and warm. Vivi hops beside me as I walk, and we slowly follow May and Batty into the house.

iii.

At lunch, I do not feel well. Mother glances at my empty plate, and then at me.

"Are you all right, Lydia?"

"I think so."

"Have some of this superb *rillette*," Father says, offering me a slice.

"Thanks, no."

May offers me the bread, brought this morning by Vivi's older sister, and I tear off a piece. I like the feel of it, textured, dusted with flour on the crusty top.

Mother sighs. "It's quiet without the children," she says. She has said this at each meal since the children left. May and I glance at each other.

"Perfect day for renting a boat," adds Father. "Nice and hot. The children loved that, the day we rented the rowboat, at the pond in Louveciennes, eh, Kate?"

The children took turns that day. Eddie and Robbie went first with Aleck, while May and Father and I stayed on the bank of the pond and helped the girls feed the fat ducks and geese, and two swans. Once Aleck brought the boat in, May took Elsie and Sister out to the center of the pond. I can still see their broad-brimmed straw hats, the picture they made. It was a bright, clear day. The pond looked as blue as lapis. I sat on a bench under the willow, playing I Spy with the boys and Aleck, as Father read the paper and Mother dozed.

Aleck has become stiffer, more formal. Marrying Lois did not help. Poor old Lois, with her aristocratic American customs and her doughy imagination. And poor Aleck too; he's caught up in that cautious, smug world, most certainly. But with each day of his visit, especially when Lois stayed in Paris and we had Aleck all to ourselves out here in the country, he seemed to become younger and more carefree. That day by the pond, he took off his shoes and socks and waded, just as we used to wade in ponds at home, catching tadpoles. I had good talks with him, over morning *café*, and sometimes in the evening as we walked in the garden. His absence feels like the violent loss of some part of me: a rib, a lung.

"I think I might walk over to see Berthe Morisot," May says, "tomorrow or the next day."

"How is her daughter?" Mother asks.

"Very well, I think."

"She must be two years old now?"

"Almost. She celebrates her birthday this fall."

"Healthy?"

"Very healthy."

"We should make a quilt for the little one, shouldn't we, Lyddy? We have the perfect material, from those two dresses you don't wear anymore. I had been about to give them away."

I nod. I hold my sides, willing my illness to go.

"Madame Manet is very lucky," Mother says. "And her child's lucky, to grow up in the country, especially in the summers."

"Country children are always the healthiest," says Father.

"Is Berthe painting again, May?" I ask.

"She writes that she's done some of the child, and the nurse."

Mother looks as if she wishes she could say something to May. I can guess what it is, and I know she feels she can no longer address the subject directly to my sister, especially now that the picture has changed, with Degas often in the foreground. She used to urge her to think about marriage, to place herself in such a way that marriage could become a possibility for her, but always May would respond high-handedly, "I'm an artist. I am independent. That's the only way a woman can do it." "You could still have your art," Mother would say, ruffled. But she didn't think of May's art as something real, something genuine. She still finds it difficult to think of May as choosing all this.

Mother still has hopes, though. I know she would love to see May situated like Berthe Morisot—Madame Manet—married to a wealthy man, well-connected. Lois too enjoys such a marriage. Aleck has become so rich.

Father, of course, agrees, and yet, ever since the Impressionist exhibition last spring, when May's paintings sold so well in spite of the critics, he seems to have begun to let the thought go. I picture him on a shore, watching a ship (*"The Marriage of My Youngest Daughter"*) sail away, just as my own ship sailed, and turning back to business. He looks at her, more and more, with simple admiration, of the kind he might feel for a manly acquaintance who's struck it rich, in railroads or in stocks.

"I can't imagine Madame Manet gets much painting done, with a small child around the house," says Father.

Mother sits up very straight. "Well, she has a nurse, after all. And she has only the one child."

"One is a handful, even with a nurse, you know that, Kate. Madame Manet certainly can't be working as hard as May does."

"I don't mean to suggest that she works as hard." Mother looks indignant. "I'm only saying, she's very fortunate to have a family, and her art too."

May sighs. "Well, she is fortunate, there's no doubt of that." She adds, sharply, "And May Alcott too was fortunate once."

Mother looks pained. She liked May Alcott, and so did I. *"This is for you, Lydia," she said, holding out a little sketchbook. "It has some sketches of you and May in it. I thought you'd like to have it." Her face a blasted winter landscape, stark white and shadowed.* May doesn't need to bring up her death so often, and with such bitterness.

"Bearing a child always carries a risk," Mother says, looking suddenly tired.

"A risk, yes." May tosses her head. "She could have become a very good painter, and then she got married, and look what happened."

I glance at May's face, furious and stubborn, and I think about how happy May Alcott was with her husband in their house in Meudon. Her baby Lulu lives in America now, with her Aunt Louisa, the writer.

"You're right, May," Mother says, "that did happen. But look at me. Five healthy children I gave birth to, and here I am still, an old woman, with healthy grandchildren."

Five healthy children, I think, *but one has been dead for more than twenty years, and another* (I put my bread on my plate) *is healthy no longer, and what about the two who did not live more than a day, or a month?*

"You never had the ambition May does, though, Kate," says Father.

"I had my own ambitions, thank you."

"Of course you did," he says, with compunction. He adds, "And you've been a model to your children."

Mother glances at him. "Well, I don't know about that. I just— it's just that having a family, and children, is natural, and good. It's a contribution in its own right." Mother's hands flutter above her plate. She touches her spoon, her white linen napkin, the asters in the vase.

I shift uncomfortably in my chair. Father shrugs his shoulders and breathes a noisy sigh, as May stabs at her salad and then lets her fork clatter onto the plate. All of us are as quiet as church, until Hélène comes in to take away the dishes and bring the fruit and cheese for dessert.

iv.

This afternoon, lying on my bed after lunch, the pain is mild, compared to last spring and other times, but I am terribly aware of my illness.

I look at the mound of books on the table. Mostly poetry, at the moment, especially that of May's friend Stéphane Mallarmé, but my head is sore. I can't imagine deciphering the words; the thought makes me nauseous.

v.

Two figures, so close I cannot distinguish them. A fabulous and strange beast, clothed and passionate. Can people's boundaries dissolve? I wonder, confused in that one slow moment.

vi.

May pokes her head around the door, and looks at me with dark eyes.

"Lyd?"

I create a smile for her.

"Yes, May."

She comes in and sits on my bed, close to me, catching up my hand. Her hands knead my fingers, as if she wishes to mold them like clay.

"You're all right?"

"Yes."

"Was it something you ate? Mother worries about the *rillette*."

"I didn't touch the *rillette*."

"You've been so well." She pauses. "Haven't you?"

"Largely, yes. I've been well."

"I know you've had trouble sleeping."

"May." I speak gently and slowly. "You know my diagnosis."

May looks impatient. "You've been fine, though, only some-times with a little sleeplessness, and then—" She studies my face.

"I know doctors can do very little. But they're not wholly ignorant."

May twists her mouth just as Mother does. It would be comical to me, if I did not feel so sorry for her, and for myself, at this moment. I glimpse May's world as it will look when I am no longer here. I do not always feel necessary—in the grand scheme of things, I feel quite unnecessary—but the picture shifts when you look through the eyes of another. I see May, sitting upright, in front of her canvas, holding her palette and her brush, and looking at—air.

And as soon as I imagine this, another picture flies into my face: *in my place is another, some young woman dressed in a dress I might have worn. On her lap is Batty, or in her hand is a crochet hook, and blue thread. She reads, or holds a cup.*

May's stubbornness on the subject of my health begins to distress me more than my diagnosis. I feel sometimes as if I'm in a rowboat, all on my own. And this is all right, if I can still see land, and houses, and my sister and others walking on the shore. But to be cut off from the shore, to have only seabirds and the impersonal sun and salty waves to witness what's happening in my boat—this is too much.

"Promise me you'll remain healthy, Lyd."

"How can I promise what I can't control?" I say, bitterly, throwing the words at her.

vii.

The woman's head turns, and I see May's face—but how could her face have arrived here, in this arbor? I feel that I've become caught in a picture, or else this picture has been thrust into my face, and I must hold my eyes open to see.

viii.

After two days, my illness subsides and I'm able to pose for May again in the garden, crocheting. On the second day, at noon, she looks up and says, with satisfaction, *"C'est fini."*

I've held off looking at the painting, this time, I'm not sure why. I'll miss this chair on the path, the garden around me, sunshine and insect murmur. Soon, these mornings in the garden at Marly will have vanished, just as the mornings and afternoons of the summer have already vanished, leaving only pictures in my memory. We'll be returning to Paris, and other people, our other life, more crowded and rushed, May darting across the city, to see friends, to go to a gallery.

"Do you like it, Lyddy?"

I look. May has created a calm scene: a woman in a garden, with a white lace bonnet and a blue dress, edged with colorful embroidery, and a dusky red row of plants behind her, leading up the *allée*, to the dark windows of the villa. She's crocheting something blue. And what is that double band of red on her lap? Ah, the sash of my dress. It startles me.

"Lyddy?"

"Oh, I do. I do like it."

May waits. I contemplate the face of this woman.

"The lines of the face—look as if they're dissolving."

"Do you like that?"

I try to smile. "Oh, May, it's magnificent. Yes. I'm amazed by those lines, her eyes, her mouth, how it's all present, and yet—"

I feel May listening hard.

"It's as if you've shown how fragile all of this is."

"All of this?"

I am embarrassed. I fling my arms out. "This garden, summer—"

May studies my face, and then she looks at the canvas.

I see something else, but I find it difficult to say this to May. *It's illness she's discovered.* I gaze at the shadows around the woman's eyes (*my eyes*), the muted color of her mouth (*my mouth*), the downturned lips. I comprehend how May sees her (*me*)—not what she acknowledges, perhaps, but what she knows.

"Do you like the light in it?"

"The light is fine."

"And her hands?"

"Yes, her hands are well done." I add, "It's a thoughtful picture."

"Thoughtful?" She moves closer to me, as she looks at her painting, as if to see it through my eyes.

"*Oui*. She's absorbed in her crocheting, but it's more than that. She looks as if she's looking inward. I suppose it's her eyes that make me think that."

May's cheek, hot and damp, touches mine, *just as on a hot Pennsylvania summer day, when she's small, and I'm carrying her somewhere. She's clinging to me, her face hot and wet on mine.*

May puts her arms around my shoulders and kisses me full on the cheek.

"Of course she's thoughtful. It's a portrait too, you know."

"I'm not so thoughtful."

"You're a contemplative, Lyddy. I've always known it about you. If you were a Catholic—God forbid!—you'd be in a nunnery."

I shake my head, but I picture with a rush of delight a cloistered garden, like the one we entered in the old *abbaye* south of Paris, stone archways, and a calm filled with something—if I were a nun I could call this thing God.

ix.

And, God in Heaven, what am I to do with this other picture, arriving in my life during one dazed moment in the middle of a summer afternoon in our garden in Marly? The woman is May—I see her face, her yellow dress. The two figures make a picture no one will paint, or see, yet it's framed, in a green like the green of the arbor, on the walls of my memory. I claim it for my own.

As May begins to put away her brushes, I catch one more glimpse of the painting.

The blood-red leaves lead to the dark windows, the red (*heart's blood*) on my dress a sash, a slash. How can May paint such darkness?

Maybe it's this talk about nunneries, but I feel a yearning for some sign—of grace, of a future life that holds more than darkened windows. Why should it be only Catholics who see such signs, like the girl who had the visions at Lourdes? I would be grateful simply for a dove, winging its careful way out of the sky. In the face of that wish, my own world seems suddenly spare and stoic and Protestant.

xi.

"Do you love him?" I ask her, as the shadows grow blue around us, once Degas has left on the train. It's August, and the air's still hot from the day. A scull passes on the river, with swift, long strokes, as the blade slices into the water again, and again. "Oh, well." I can just see her shrugging, tossing her hands into the air. "Do you?" I ask again. She hugs her elbows, and looks at the water, and then she comes closer.

"I'm overwhelmed by him."

"Do you intend to marry?"

She laughs and I think she's mocking me, but then she says fiercely, "I couldn't marry him, Lyddy. You of all people know that. How could I? He would crush my painting, me. I couldn't possibly survive it."

"Then what in Heaven's name are you thinking?" I ask, in anguish.

"I can't say what I'm thinking, Lyddy, but I can't bear to feel I can't have this in my life, ever. This is not Philadelphia. Am I to live with no feeling, like—?"

Like you, she almost says, and I feel the cut of her words against my face.

"I'm not asking you to live with no feeling, May," I begin, and at once I'm aware how my own life must look in her eyes, a desert, parched under a hot sun.

Her arm around his neck, her face joyous

And—"Lyddy. You must try to understand."

xii.

As I stand now in the hot sun on the *allée*, contemplating May's picture, I almost shake with sorrow and fury. I don't want to give any of this up: May's cheek, this light, the possibility of love. How can this be asked of me? I'm only beginning to understand how to live. And here is May, her life in full flush, a success now, and healthy, and boldly independent. And she will continue, for years and years, after I'm no longer here. She'll ride her horse in the Bois de Boulogne, she'll paint and visit galleries and go to the Opéra and to Versailles, and in the summer she'll come back to Marly, or she'll go to the Mediterranean and feel the breezes, watch the water turn color through a whole day, a whole week, and she'll have her friends, and more than friends, for after Edgar Degas, she may love someone else, and embrace him in another garden, and even if I am a thought in her mind, a sadness, she will have happiness too. Her days glitter, round and new, like gold coins in a huge jar, filled almost to the brim, her only worry how to spend them.

May threads her arm through mine, and we walk toward the villa, my heart like hot sand. May carries her case of paints and brushes, and I carry my crochet hook and the blue shawl for Corabella, strangely heavy now for such a small thing.

"I have to live my life as it comes to me, Lyddy, I can't be always waiting. You can't know how it is."

But I do, I think. I do.

Driving

then I'm in a garden at the abbaye, *and I see May, painting a woman in a yellow dress, and I call to her but she does not hear me,*

i.

"But I can't believe she would sell it." Mother looks at me in aston-ishment. She's come into my room, after breakfast. I've just begun Henry James' novel, *The American*, and I put it down reluctantly.

"Well, it is art, after all. It's a beautiful painting."

This is the twentieth conversation I've had with Mother on this subject, ever since Moïse Dreyfus bought one of May's family paintings, the one of Mother reading fairy tales to Elsie and Sister and Robbie last summer in Marly. Our household has flown into a whirlwind of emotion over this, like a hen house visited by a fox. Feathers fly everywhere. In a larger sense, I think, May's recent suc-cess is the fox, or maybe May herself. The *6ème* Impressionist exhi-bition, which opened in April on the boulevard des Capucines, has been a triumph, especially for May and Edgar Degas. She's gar-nered excellent reviews, and has had offers on all eleven of her entries. People are saying she'll never have to worry now about whether she'll be able to sell her art, and at a good price too. "Too much pudding," May says, daily, about all the praise and attention, but I know she's delighted—more than delighted. Victorious.

"Yes, but Lydia, how could she sell her own mother, and her nieces and nephew?"

"She's not selling you! She's selling a painting of you! There's a difference, I hope."

"It's a painting of my grandchildren and me. How could she possibly think of earning money for it, and losing it to someone outside the family?"

I sigh. How, indeed?

"At least she won't be selling the three of you, Lydia."

I picture those: the one of me holding the cup of tea, and the one in the garden at Marly, and another one, a profile of me on the green bench in the Bois de Boulogne, with my black bonnet and the red trim. I look sober in that one, my lips a tight line, as May poses me looking off into the distance, with my coat a swirl of crazed autumn colors.

"Well, she's not selling them yet, at any rate," I say.

"How can you say that! Surely she'll never let those go."

"But art isn't made simply for one's family. It's for others to see too."

"Yes, and I wish others to honor her accomplishment. But she must honor our wishes also. A portrait of her mother should be returned to her family."

"I agree with you. I wish May would too. But she has her own point of view. She's an artist. She wishes her work to be out in the world."

"But it's a betrayal, Lyddy. Surely you see that. She betrays me, and you, all of us, by sending our pictures into the marketplace like this. Who is going to care about such pictures as much as Mary's own family?"

In the painting of Mother and the children, May shows them wrapped together in the beauty of the afternoon, the magic of the story. I have to agree, it's hard to think of that little band hanging on a wall in Moïse Dreyfus's house, adding to his collection. I had not realized the extent of May's ambition.

Yet I have become aware, too, of how I have contributed to her success. The pictures she painted of me have brought especially high offers, and immense praise. When people think of her art now, they think of me, although they may have no idea who I am.

May is home this morning, a Sunday morning. We've been making plans with Mother and Father for our move to a summer house in Louveciennes in a few weeks. Our younger brother Gard will be coming to visit, and I can't wait to see him.

"I have a new idea for you, Lyddy." May says this hesitantly, as she pours herself another cup of *café*.

"Tell me."

"A painting outdoors, in the Bois. With figures in a carriage." She looks at me hopefully.

"With Bichette?"

May laughs. "Yes, of course, Bichette. The carriage must have a horse."

"And—someone in the carriage?"

"Could it be you, Lyddy? I'm thinking of you, driving, with a little girl, and maybe Mathieu could be in it too, as the groom."

I try to picture this. I've seen some unusual pictures of Edgar Degas'—fashionable people near a racecourse. May has painted her own horse only rarely. "Who would the child be? Do you have a model?"

May looks into her cup. "Well, I know of one."

"Who is it?"

May looks at me quickly, her face flushing. "A little niece of Edgar's. Odile. Odile Fèvre."

"How old is she?"

"I think she's about five. She has a hint of baby plumpness still, and honey-colored hair."

"Her mother is Edgar's sister?"

"*Oui*. Marguerite."

"I thought Madame Fèvre had moved to South America?"

"Buenos Aires. She and Henri moved there two years ago. She's just visiting now, with her children."

"How many children does she have?"

"Five. Odile's the youngest."

"And will Odile come with her mother?"

"I think so, usually." May's flush deepens. "More *café*?"

"Thanks, yes."

As May pours the *café* into my cup, she studies my face. "So— will you pose for this one, Lyddy?"

The cup feels hot in my hands. I breathe in the fragrance, as I think about how I yearn to pose again, especially with this child. It's a kind of hunger. Yet I've been more under the weather than usual.

"My health has been so uncertain," I begin.

May interrupts me. "I know, Lyddy, *mais*—" She pauses, then adds, looking away, "*J'ai besoin de toi*. I need you. It's as simple as that. The picture I conceive of has you in it. Most of my pictures do, these days."

I look at May quickly, my eyes stinging. I am surprised, and moved, by her sense of such necessity. I realize suddenly that she must wonder, as I do, how much time I have left. And I realize too that I would regret each day I refused her. To refuse to pose is a form of betrayal. I study May's anxious face.

"And if I become sick while you're trying to paint me?"

"I'll figure out something. I'm very resourceful. Let's not court disaster, anyway, Lyd."

I taste the *café*, and add some milk, as I contemplate the difficult walk down five flights of stairs, the ride to the Bois, the long hours posing, the ascent, once more, of stair after stair. And I contemplate, too, the day I won't be able to rise from my bed.

"*D'accord*, May."

"Can you begin tomorrow?"

"Tomorrow. *Oui*."

iii.

This morning Odile comes to the Bois with her mother. May and I wait with Mathieu in a quiet part of the park, to the side of a gravelled *allée*. To our right is a stand of trees, and to our left, a large open lawn. A short drive would bring us to the café, and the lake, where children throw bits of bread into the water and sail their boats. May and I used to go there often on summer evenings for ices, with Louie Elder and other friends—May Alcott too, so pretty and happy. Colored lights threaded through the trees, above the noisy crowd.

Here, though, on this *allée*, all is quiet. Swallows skim the grass, and I spot a hawk too, soaring above the meadow. I wonder what it sees, with its sharp eyes: a mouse, a snake, a family of partridges?

The sun grows warm, and as I sit in the carriage I hold my white lace parasol over my head. May walks restlessly along the lane, shading her eyes now and again, looking for Madame Fèvre. Mathieu stands by Bichette, holding the reins and looking quite grand, in the black silk hat and frock coat May has borrowed for him, his ears sticking out, his fair face freckled.

After a while, a cab comes along, with two horses. The driver slows as he nears us, and in a moment a woman in a sherry-colored dress steps out, and then a little girl. The child wears a pink and white summer dress with short sleeves, and a black straw hat. Her hair tumbles in waves down her back, the color of taffy. May rushes to greet them. I see her bend down to talk to the little girl.

The girl holds her mother's gloved hand in her own bare one, and they walk toward me.

iv.

Posing in the carriage next to Odile, I think about how she has, not an ordinary beauty, but something more inward. She makes me think of Elsie, although Elsie would never sit still for an hour at a time. I discover something touching in this child's politeness.

May is talking to Marguerite, in French.

"Will you stay in Paris for the whole summer, *madame?*"

"I hope so, *mademoiselle*. I have missed Paris."

"And Buenos Aires? Do you like it there?"

"Buenos Aires is unusual. It's pretty, in parts. And Henri has found much to do, with all the new building."

"Your husband is an architect?

"*Oui.*"

"And your children—they like it too?"

"Do you like our home, in Buenos Aires, *ma petite?*" Marguerite asks her daughter.

"*Oui, bien sûr, maman*. I love my room there, and my parrot. And I love our orange tree."

Woman and Child Driving, Philadephia Museum of Art: The W. P. Wilstach Collection.

"You have an orange tree in your garden?" I ask, wishing I could turn my head to look at her.

"*Oui, mademoiselle.* My parrot often sits in the orange tree. He says, *'Buenos dias,'* and he calls for me when I'm not there. He opens his beak wide and cries, *'Odile! Odile!'* He does not cry for my sisters, oh no, that's certain."

"Keep still, Odile! Mademoiselle Cassatt is painting a picture of you, remember!"

"Your parrot speaks Spanish?" I ask my companion.

"*Oui, mademoiselle,* Spanish and French. I am going to teach him English too."

"Better learn English yourself first, *ma chérie,*" Marguerite says, laughing.

"Oncle Edgar will teach me English, and then I will teach it to my parrot."

"I'm teaching myself English," pipes up Mathieu. I had forgotten his presence behind us, on the back seat, facing backwards. "I am going to America one day," he announces.

"And what will you do in America, Mathieu?" May asks.

"I'll stay in a hotel in New York, and then I'll go all across the country, to San Francisco, *mademoiselle.*"

"You've been thinking about this a lot, I see!" May says, and I can tell she's smiling. She likes Mathieu. "And what will you do in San Francisco?"

"I'll gaze at the Pacific Ocean!"

"And you will be happy?"

"*Oui, mademoiselle.* Very happy!"

"Ah, lucky Mathieu, to have such a dream!"

v.

I am aware of the day's warmth, and of Odile's shoulder touching my arm. My arms ache as I hold the reins and the whip. I wish I could take off my hat and my scarf.

As I pose, I wonder what people think of us, as they pass in their carriages or on horseback. When the *allée* is quiet, I can almost imagine that we're in West Chester, or at our beautiful old country house, Hardwicke. Looking at the lawn out of the corner of my eye, I can dream that it's the first meadow behind the house, where Aleck and I would ride. The *bois*, too, could be the woods around the rim of the pastures, dark and inviting, where we explored, playing wild Indians.

Clouds begin to enter the sky, at first just white ones, then tinged with gray.

"I hope it doesn't rain," May says.

When the sky whitens and the sun vanishes, the air begins to feel like cotton, thick and full. May tries to engage all of us in conversation, but her voice sounds oddly distant, and I am tired. Odile has become as quiet as a pond.

Odile moves slightly on the seat, and sighs.

"You must sit still, Odile," her mother says.

When Batty barks at something (*tin tin tin*), the child starts, and out of the corner of my eye I can see that she's turned her head to look at him. Then she says, in a small voice, that her head has an itch.

"*Alors*, take care of your head, then," her mother says, "but *vite, vite!* Mademoiselle Cassatt is painting an important picture."

"May I see it, *mademoiselle?*" Odile asks. I can tell she's removed her hat in order to scratch her head.

"*Bientôt*," says May.

The clouds cover the sun completely, and the trees bend in the suddenly cool breeze. I shiver, even though I'm wearing such a heavy dress, with a jacket, and my bonnet with fur trim, my long gloves.

"Perhaps the child is cold, May?" I say.

"I'm almost done for the morning," May says. She adds, "Are you cold, Odile?"

"*Oui, mademoiselle, un peu.*"

"Well, just a little more, and then you can chase Batty. Do you like dogs?"

"*Oui, mademoiselle.*"

When May releases us, Odile jumps off the carriage, and Batty runs to her, barking. She bends down to him, and lets him lick her face. Mathieu stretches, and takes off his top hat, loosens his collar. Marguerite smooths Odile's hair, and gives her a kiss, and in a moment we squeeze back into the carriage, laughing, and Mathieu drives all of us to the café, for *pâtisseries*. It's like a holiday, with Batty on my lap, May's canvas and paints stuffed under the seat, Odile on her mother's lap, and Mathieu, his silk hat cocked rakishly off his forehead, driving us through a tunnel of trees as the sun begins to shine again, in dappled patterns, on the *allée*.

On the second day of our posing in the Bois, the sky burns blue, and the sun shines with summer strength.

I am sitting in the carriage, fanning myself, with Mathieu behind me, when Odile arrives at our spot with her Oncle Edgar. She skips at his side, and when she says *"Bonjour, mademoiselle,"* to me, she smiles. She laughs when she sees Batty. Turning to her uncle, she asks, "May I give him something I saved from my breakfast?"

Edgar glances, amused, at May, and says, "Better ask Batty's mistress."

Odile shows May a tiny strawberry, half mashed from being held in her hand.

"Of course!" May says. "Batty adores strawberries."

"I thought so." Odile nods. "My dog adores them too." She tosses the strawberry into the air, and Batty catches it neatly in his mouth, eyes glittering.

"Now let's see about your hand, *ma petite.*" Edgar draws a hand-kerchief out of his pocket, and rubs her hand briskly. "You're full of surprises, aren't you? I had no idea you'd been holding that straw-berry in your hand all the way from the hotel."

"We're only staying in the hotel for one more week," Odile

confides to May, "and then we go to my Tante Thérèse, and after that to the seashore, for the air."

"How splendid," May says, setting up her paints. She drops a brush, and Edgar bends to pick it up. As he hands it to her, slowly, the breeze stills, and the grass seems to shimmer with heat. The lawn, with its running slope, surrounds these two figures with green-gold. May stands close to Edgar, the hem of her blue skirt almost touching his cane. I feel bereft, suddenly, or as if I have become a spirit merely, my flesh melted away; I gaze at my sister and Edgar, and I know I am outside the picture.

In another instant, Edgar calls to Odile, and holds her hand as they walk to the carriage. Mathieu jumps onto the carriage behind me, and Edgar says "Up we go!" and lifts Odile into the air, her pink dress fluttering like a banner.

As he places Odile on the seat, smoothing her dress, he glances at me, and, as quickly as a cat's paw on a meadow, something passes between us, in this bright air. He looks at me as if he knows me, as if he has discovered what I know, and also what I desire.

As we pose, and white clouds sail across the sky and then vanish from my sight, I grow hot in my dress.

"Lyddy!" May's voice startles me.

"Yes?"

"You look half asleep, and Odile too."

"I am sleepy," agrees Odile.

"Can you think of a story to tell, Lyd? I've forgotten the book of fairy tales I meant to bring."

"I can't think of a story, May."

"Then Monsieur Degas will have to think of one."

"*Oui*, Oncle Edgar! Tell them about your journey to Italy, when you were little. Tell them about how you learned to swim, in the stream outside of Naples, and how your brother Achille fell in and almost drowned."

"What a memory you have! Who told you that story?" Degas laughs.

"You did! Just last week!"

"Ah! Well. I think that story must be too sad, or else too boring."

"*Mais non!* It's a good story. You rescued Achille, don't you remember?"

"Ah, yes. Well, either I did, or our tutor. He ended up rather wet, I think, but he was a good type, and we had a splashing fight, while Achille sat on the bank covered in towels, and I defeated my tutor utterly, something he was quite used to, in fact."

"I wish I could swim here," says Odile. "Maybe in the duck pond."

"The duck pond is filthy, *mon chou*. A *gendarme* would fish you out, in any case, and reprimand you severely."

"I would slip away from him, then, and find another place to swim."

"You are a person of exceptional vision and courage, Odile," her uncle says.

viii.

By the time May lets us rest, I am overwhelmed by the heat.

Edgar helps Odile out, and then, with unusual gentleness, he offers me his hand, and I slowly move to the edge of the carriage. He holds my arm as I come down the step.

"You look tired," he says.

"Sit on the blanket, Lyddy," May says, spreading our old picnic blanket with the Scottish plaid on the edge of the lawn. "Mathieu! Go to the café, and buy some camembert and bread. Oh, and see if they have a good pâté, maybe some *saucisson*. We'll have a splendid picnic."

She gives him money. Mathieu looks relieved to stretch, and

then to jump into the driver's seat and flick the whip, touching Bichette's rump.

"Chocolate too, Mathieu!" May calls to him. "And cider!"

"*D'accord, mademoiselle,*" Mathieu shouts, as the carriage rumbles down the *allée*, a cloud of dust blooming behind it.

"I see myself!" says Odile. She's gazing at May's picture. "See my pink dress? And my shoes? I am very, very quiet, aren't I?"

"You are the queen of quietness," says Edgar.

"Mademoiselle Cassatt too," Odile says.

"Mademoiselle Cassatt is astonishingly quiet as well."

Looking at Degas, I am aware of his eyes upon me. He seems to slice through my skin, layer after layer. *So now we know something of each other's secrets,* he seems to say, his eyes dark, inquisitive. *Yes.*

Sitting on the blanket, I can see the picture on May's easel. It has a darkness I had not anticipated. I recognize myself, and Odile, and Mathieu, yet we look odd, somber, as if on a grim errand. Each of us stares in a different direction, but we don't look as if we're really seeing anything. The luscious colors of Odile's face and hair and dress make a splash of brightness, but surrounding her loom darker colors: the black and dusky red of my bonnet, the various blacks of Mathieu's hat

125

and coat, Bichette's tail, the whip. In the background, the trees, which in reality (I glance at them now) look so welcoming and summery, with their crowns of green, appear shadowy. And I look solemn and determined, stoical, as I stare straight ahead, holding the reins and the whip. Of course, the picture is not finished.

I see this painting, suddenly, as a message from May to me. *I know you're on a journey*, the painting says, *to another, darker place. And even though you betray me by leaving, I grant you companions—a child, a groom—to accompany you when I cannot follow. I cannot make your journey joyous, but I promise at least to record your passage.*

May and Edgar sit next to each other, on the other side of the blanket, as Odile comes racing past us, Batty at her heels. When Mathieu returns, he hands the lunch to May, then tosses Batty a stick. May tears the bread, and Edgar opens a pocket knife to cut into the round of cheese. I pour the cider into our glasses.

As I eat the camembert on bread, and taste the delicious little pickles, *cornichons*, I gaze at May's painting. She has pictured something red flowing out of my heart. I look down at my silk jacket and my scarf. They hold different shades of red, yes, but May has changed these reds into something other than a jacket or a scarf, something pouring, a river, with tributaries. And here, around my dress, just under my knees, she's painted a second ribbon of crimson, and on Odile's dress too, bands of another shade, the red of mashed strawberries.

My cider spills in the grass. I right my glass, and rise, moving slowly, as if through water, toward the carriage, hoping to open my parasol. Perhaps this nausea and dizziness come only from the heat.

"Mademoiselle Cassatt! *Vous voyez?* See how Batty can jump!"

I try to smile at Odile as she holds up a stick for Batty, and then the sky, and the trees, and May, and the others, seem to swirl upside down, and I discover that I have collapsed to my knees in the *allée*.

ix.

At home, I am ill again, very ill. I am barely aware who sits next to me in my bedroom. It must be May. I know her touch. I see the deep blue of her dress, but I feel too sick to look at her. She brings me the basin, when I ask her, and she smooths my hair as I open, like a sluice. I am in pain. I am in pain. God help me.

Outside my window, over the sounds of the avenue, I think I hear a child's voice, like the cry of a strange bird, high and floating.

127

Shadows hover in my room, deep black, gray, even red. I had not thought shadows could come in so many colors.

Lyddy, someone says. It's Mother. Her hand is cool and soft on my forehead. Are you are you all right. I shake my head and I begin to cry. Do you feel pain. Pain. Yes. Shall I call the doctor. What can a doctor do.

Hours pass, days, and I wake to see a girl with taffy-colored hair by my bed. Is this a dream? I wonder, but then I know she is Odile. She wears her hat and a white coat, and gloves. In the shadows stands Edgar. I hope you recover soon, he says to me. Your sister is at a loss without you. I try to smile but my face won't bend that way anymore, and I say, Are you well? And he says, oui, and I ask the child too if she's well, and she says oui, mademoiselle. She holds out a bunch of red tulips, and May takes them, or is it Mother, and says thank you, ma petite, she will love these when she's feeling well enough to gaze at them, and when I look again, Edgar and the child have gone.

I see Thomas, in the afternoon light, sitting calmly at the foot of my bed, gazing at me. You're not dead, then? I ask, bewildered, and he smiles. Well, you see me, don't you? he asks. Yes, I see you. He laughs and shrugs, ordinary and handsome as the day. Bending closer, he asks, Then what is death?

I open my eyes to see May sitting on my bed, dark circles under her eyes. I hold still, waiting for the pain, but for the moment the pain is not here.

"Is it morning?"

"*Oui.*"

"Have I been sick long?"

"*Oui.* Days."

"And—" I hesitate. "Is Odile all right?"

"Of course she is."

"Will she come back?"

"One day, I'm sure. Marguerite decided to take them south, to Nice."

"But the painting?"

"I've finished it."

"How?"

"Well, I painted your face, actually, most of you, before you fell ill, Lyddy, remember? And Mathieu and Odile posed for another couple of days."

"Who held the reins?"

"Louie did. She came with us, to help me finish."

"So—it's done?"

"Yes."

"*Et*—do you like it?"

May looks sad. "I do like it."

"I know it must have come out well, May." *from my heart, a river of red, mute, terrifying*

"Yes. And now you must get better."

But this is a task I seem to have forgotten how to do.

May draws open the curtains, and the light hurts my eyes. How long has it been since I have seen light?

I think of the painting.

And am I on a journey, then? And who goes with me?

xi.

In the afternoon, before May returns, the bell rings, and in a moment I hear Mother talking to someone.

"Degas is here," she says, poking her head into my room. "Would you be able to come say hello?"

The idea of walking from one room to another overwhelms

me, and I feel unnerved, too, at the thought of facing Edgar on my own, without May. I'm not sure why I feel this. I shake my head, and Mother's face disappears.

In a moment, she pokes her head into my room again.

"Could he come in here to see you, Lyddy, just for a moment?"

I hesitate. I must look awful, raggedy and pale; I haven't had a real bath in days.

"I—" I look around my small room, and touch my hand to my hair.

Mother guesses part of my panic. She brushes my hair, sweeping it into a simple *chignon*, and brings me a fresh cap. Then she helps me sit up, and wraps my white shawl around my bed jacket.

When Edgar comes in, Mother gives him the armchair by my bed, and she sits on the ottoman by my dressing table. Looking slightly awkward, beneath his usual ironic pose, he studies my face. For once, to my surprise, I welcome his look. I realize with a stumble of my own heart that I wish to be seen by someone who can see with clarity.

Mother and Edgar chat about his family. When Mother leaves the room for a moment to find her sewing, I look at him. My shyness slips off, like a dress, to the floor around me, something I used to wear.

"You're better?" he asks.

"*Oui, pour le moment.*"

He considers my words.

"A moment can hold great value."

"I wish for more than that."

"Of course you do. Who would not wish for more?"

My eyes sting.

"My family finds it hard to acknowledge how little time I might have. I think May's beginning to acknowledge it."

"*Et toi?* Do you find it hard to acknowledge as well?"

"I don't want to vanish."

"Vanish? *Mais*, the vanishing isn't the point, is it?"

I rub my cheek fiercely. I do not wish to cry. "What's the point then?"

He shrugs. "Seeing. Creating something." He catches my eye now, and holds my gaze. "You do that. You know that, more than most of these types of humanity. You see things, I can tell." *Her arm around his neck, two figures embracing. I claim this picture for my own.* He adds, "You've given more than you may know to your sister."

I have come to a new landscape with this man, a sober place, without many trees. The light shines strongly here, and yet much is in shade. It is not a desert, yet the desire for water, I know, will not be fully satisfied.

"I love her," I say.

"Oui, évidemment, and you give her something else, too. You give her—" He pauses, searching for words. "A sense of something terribly valuable, something she must work her way towards, in paint."

"And that's good?"

Edgar laughs a short, sharp laugh. "Good? Oui, c'est bien. All of us need something to work towards—to claw our way to, if necessary—to crawl on our bellies to, through mud and across stones, in order to touch and understand a mere part of it."

"But I wish for this myself," I say, astonished at my fierceness. "I wish to be the one clawing, and crawling, surging toward something I love and wish to have."

Naked, this look between us, unhinged. Edgar seems to listen to what I can't say, how I wish to live, to enter the arbor, to swim into the kiss, to break my pose and walk into my own life.

"How do you know you don't?" he asks with quick urgency, his voice low. "How do you know you don't labor towards something? You seem like one who must know about such effort."

"I'm dying."

"Oui. I know."

"And I haven't created anything. I have nothing to leave behind me."

"But you allow yourself to be in the picture."

133

"That's different." My voice sounds harsh, broken.

"Is it? I wonder. And besides, one can labor towards something that never becomes art, or even visible. But you can have it in here." He touches his eyes, and then he bends closer and says, quietly, "You know, you're the one she loves most in the world. She will never love another as well. How can you say you leave nothing behind?" He moves back into his chair, and gazes at me with dark eyes. "You're magnificent, after all."

I let his words float in the air, fall around me, like cherry blossoms. *N'importe quoi*, I would say to anyone else, at any other time, but in this dream-like moment, in this desert, blooming, I accept the words as an unanticipated gift.

Degas rubs his eyes, and I think of something May told me a couple of weeks ago.

"His eyes are bad."

"Bad?"

"He can't see well. When he looks at something, he can't see the center."

"How can that be? He paints. He paints constantly."

May looks at me soberly and shrugs. "Of course he paints."

"But—what will happen?"

"I don't know. He thinks he may go blind."

Lydia Seated at an Embroidery Frame

and then I'm holding a small May's hand, and we're in the meadow behind our house at Hardwicke, and we walk through the high grass, among the fireflies, through the gate and past the barn, and the garden, toward the house, and I can see light inside, and Ella's at the front door, waving us in for bed, and

i.

Sewing the piece of silk onto my embroidery frame after breakfast, I picture Elsie's clear eyes.

"What do you think Elsie would like on her pillowcase?" I call to Mother, who's reading the paper in her bedroom.

Mother comes slowly to my door. I hear her slippered steps on the rug, her sighs.

"Have you looked in those, Lyddy?" She motions toward my pattern-box and the magazines piled on my dressing table.

"I've looked through everything."

"You might try flowers again." Mother plumps herself on my bed and takes off her specs, cleaning them with her shawl.

"Elsie's can't look too much like Sister's, though." For Sister, I embroidered a pillowcase with a border of roses, twining, *like the roses in the arbor, one hot day in August, scorching, fragrant.*

139

"What about wildflowers?"

"Wildflowers. Yes." Perfect, I think, for isn't Elsie just like a wildflower, brightly colored and uncultivated? I wish children could always stay that way. May is more like that, still, than most women I've ever known. I remember, last summer, how Elsie couldn't restrain herself from picking the flowers in the garden. May and I took her to the riverbank and let her gather bunches of wildflowers, instead, and grass too, which seemed to Elsie as splendid as flowers.

"I know American wildflowers best, though," I say.

"Well, Elsie's an American, through and through," Mother says drily. "I still have my book of American wildflowers." She pushes herself off the bed, and walks slowly out of my room. "I'll find it for you."

As I pore over the pictures in her book, I relish the flowers' names, the way they seem to sing and to bite: trillium, columbine, dog-tooth violet. I yearn suddenly for my sketchbook, the one in which I drew wildflowers in pen and watercolor the summer I agreed to marry Thomas. I wonder if Mother still has it, stowed away in a chest, here or in America, or if it sits somewhere among Aleck's papers.

I mark the wildflowers I like best, and then I begin to sketch a design on paper. I want something modern, not old-fashioned—a clean, spare form. I toss out design after design. I'll know the right one when it comes to me.

Our apartment feels quiet today. Father has gone riding, and Mother is reading now in her room. May is at her studio, I think (*and who is with her? and what do they do? I picture Edgar lounging on the chair near her, smoking, rubbing his eyes, the pigeons whirring, May talking to her new model*).

Today I feel as if I have fallen out of the whole picture. Sometimes, this morning, I have the sense of foreknowledge: *this is how the world will be when you are no longer here. This is how it will go on without you.* I wish to throw my arms around the day, embrace it fiercely, make it impossible for it to let me go.

That afternoon, a month ago, when Edgar Degas came to my bedside, he seemed to offer me a picture of myself, one to strive towards. In this picture, I possessed grace and strength and valor. And he had the kindness to claim that it was I who had presented him with such a vision. *"You show me how to live,"* he said, *"if only I could do it as you do."*

One June afternoon, I begin my stitching on Elsie's silk. I try to pour all my thoughts into this one task, this here and now. I've been so ill this month that I'm beginning to wonder whether I'll ever pose for May again, or whether she'll even ask me.

I've designed seven circles, to be stitched in a grass-green running stitch, on the white ground, each one framing a wildflower. I've chosen flowers I hope Elsie will recognize: buttercups, Indian paintbrush, wild sweet William, clover, pink lady's slippers, bee balm, wild columbine.

I hear May open the front door. She comes into my room as I'm threading the needle with a yellow silk, to begin the buttercups. She looks as if she's run up the five flights of stairs to our apartment.

"You're home early."

"Yes, I am."

May pulls off her burgundy gloves and lays them over the wooden bar of my embroidery frame. She looks hot.

"Did you go to the gallery?"

"Yes. I saw some good things there. I'll have to bring Louie back with me and urge her to buy something. Renoir has a new one for sale, and Camille Pissarro has some good things."

"*Et* Degas?"

May touches my embroidery frame. "Degas has a stunning pastel. I should buy it, just so you can see it. I'm thinking of urging Louie to buy it."

She looks over my shoulder.

"Oh, Lyddy, I like your design."

I hear a new note in May's voice: sorrow, is it? or just tiredness? She walks about my room, touching my hairbrush, smoothing my bed, straightening my books.

"You're reading Tennyson?" she asks, opening a little gold book.

"Yes."

"Ah! 'The Lotos-Eaters.'"

She sits in the armchair by my bed and begins to read.

After a while I ask, "What are you painting these days, May?"

She looks up and shrugs. "Oh, not much. I started another picture, with a friend of Louie's as a model, but it didn't go well."

"Are you sure?"

"It was all right, just—a bit flat. I'm looking for a new idea, really."

"And your prints?"

"I'm tired of prints, for the moment."

May reads, as I stitch one of my buttercups.

"Lyddy."

143

I look up.

"Could I paint you again?"

Her question almost makes me tremble, I'm not sure why.

"I look dreadful."

"How can you say that? You look just like yourself."

"I have no color."

"You're simply fair." May gives me a teasing smile. "I'll give you color, *de toute manière.*"

"I feel so heavy, May, you've no idea. I'm like a hippopotamus in my slowness, these days. I'm not sure I could even walk as far as your studio. I have such stupid aches."

"I can paint you right here, then."

"*Ici?*"

"In your room."

"*Mais*—the oil paints will smell, won't they? And there's hardly space enough." I look around my room.

"The smell won't be so bad. We'll air it out each day, afterward. And I can manage with the space."

I look at her face, the shadows under her eyes.

"Do you have no other model right now, May?"

"Of course I have other models. It's you I want. I've been dreaming about this picture, Lyddy, of you at your embroidery."

You allow yourself to be in the picture. A sense of something terribly valuable.
"All right. I will."

"*Merci.*" May embraces me hard. "Do you think you could begin tomorrow morning?"

"Tomorrow morning, yes."

May rises and opens my wardrobe. She sifts through my dresses.

"And—could you wear this dress?" She holds up my salmon-pink silk with the high collar and the flower-print.

"*Bien sûr,* of course I will."

iii.

In the morning, after breakfast, I put on my salmon-pink dress, and arrange my hair, and then I look at the buttercups I stitched yesterday. I can picture Elsie tracing the green stems and the buttery flowers, with her finger, before she sleeps on a hot summer's night, when the light still holds on the lawn outside her window, or on a night in the middle of winter, when all the world seems hoary and blank, and her pillow is a field.

Remember me, I wish to say to this young niece. *Don't allow me to be forgotten.* And isn't this what I wish to say to May, and to others? To

Edgar too, the one I had always thought of as merely brutal, whose kindness shimmers, in a certain light, like quick gold brushstrokes touching his shoulders, his face, throwing one utterly off guard. *You're magnificent, he said, and I thought in that instant, to my great surprise, if I could love anyone now, it would be this man, arrogant and imperfect as he is, for in that moment, in our strange landscape, I felt shaken, touched, as if he had opened up my very flesh. I know this is not love as May knows it, but it is a kind of love, springing from some hard truth, gazed at together, truth and longing.*

When May comes in with her easel, I notice her burgundy gloves, still draped over the frame.

"Shouldn't you move your gloves, May?"

May follows my glance to the frame.

"I had forgotten the gloves, but actually, I like them there, Lyd. I think they add something."

I shrug. As May sets up her easel, and prepares to paint, I thread my needle with a light blue floss, for the wild sweet William, and begin a fishbone stitch for the petals. Each small flower has five petals, like five slender blue hearts, and all of these flowers together create a burst of color.

I almost hold my breath as I try the first few stitches. I can never be sure if my design will come out right. The color shines against the white ground, and in a few minutes I can see that the petals, although simple, will look much like the myriad petals of a sweet William.

iv.

"Could you hold your hands still for a moment, Lyddy?"

I hold still, gazing at my right hand, held just above the silk, in the act of pushing the needle through. The needle shines, silvery, in my fingers. Mother's porcelain thimble crowns my second finger. The silk is pierced by silver. I keep my left hand still, just under the cloth, holding the needle as it comes through beneath.

May sits so close to me that I can hear the smallest rustle of her skirt. Her lemony cologne mingles with the stronger smell of the oils.

When Edgar visits, in the late morning, he looks hot and winded. As I break my pose, I can see his damp shirt beneath his summer coat. I feel a kind of humming inside me.

"Your sister told me you were posing for her again," he says. "I wished to see for myself."

I smile, and my face grows hot. *And are you in love, then?* I ask myself. *And what do you expect to happen? Nothing. Nothing. Only this, his eyes upon me, the air between us quickly threaded through with something blue, gold, barely visible. I can have this much.*

May is looking at me, curious. She looks as if she's forgotten what she's doing, why she's here. She almost asks me something, but then seems to think better of it.

All I can think is that this humming is something I acknowledge and accept. I am guilty of nothing more.

Degas tosses himself into the chair by my bed, as May helps me find my pose again. She touches my shoulder—"Good, Lyd"—and then my chin—"*C'est bien.*" Before she moves away, she holds her hand to my cheek. Her hand is warm, and I am for a dazed moment on a lawn in Pennsylvania with May, *her small hand hot on my cheek, as she turns my face toward her to gain my attention. Lyddy.*

I feel my face hot, still, as I look at my embroidery, the needle threaded with a rich purple for the wild columbine. I make a few stitches with the floss, hoping I can fill in one part of this upside-down flower, this gay plumage, fool's cap, before May asks me to hold my pose.

"Would you like me to read?" Edgar asks. "How about this? Tennyson?"

Lydia at a Tapestry Frame, Collection of the Flint Institute of Arts, Gift of the Whiting Foundation, 1967.32.

I know May will ask for "The Lady of Shalott," and she does. It was her favorite when she was little. Tennyson's words, in Degas' voice and accent, seem to break off bits of color, the rhymes sweeping the colors into arcs, as strong as nets.

She left the web, she left the loom,
She made three paces through the room,
She saw the water-lily bloom,
She looked down to Camelot.

I used to love this poem, although I find it a bit sillier now, too romantic and melodramatic, and Edgar seems to think so too, for he adds a touch of mockery to his reading, undercutting Tennyson's sense of tragedy, as the Lady sings her dying song, on her way to Camelot, heartsick for love of Lancelot. Yet, as Edgar reaches the end, his voice becomes more serious. May and I join him for the last lines, from memory.

He said, 'She has a lovely face;
God in his mercy lend her grace,
The Lady of Shalott.'

The poem floats in the room.

"*Pas mal,*" Edgar says. I look at my fingers, pushing the needle through, with the deep purple thread. I wish I could see his face. I feel his eyes on me, scraping and gentle, grave and amused, passionate and objective.

"You must wish for a rest, Lyddy?" May asks.

"I'm all right," I say, but I think, *No, it's not rest I desire, but to be here, with this light, this needle, these eyes.*

vii.

After tea, May dresses, to see friends, she says, at the Comédie Française. I picture Edgar, sitting just behind her, half in shadow.

After writing a letter to each of Aleck's children, I stand in the lamplight, in my bare feet and robe, looking at the painting May has begun of me. It's already a striking picture, showing a woman behind an embroidery frame, sewing, her head bent forward. A waterfall of white splashes on the left side of the canvas—the curtain, that must be. May has made a line, in gold, along my neck and shoulder, and my right arm. She has brought the most detail to my face so far. But what is that splash of deep burgundy, almost black, near the middle of the picture? Looking at my embroidery frame, I see May's new gloves lying peacefully over the top.

a sense of something terribly valuable

In bed, I open my Tennyson to "Tithonus." A luscious, slow-moving poem, a love-poem of sorts.

   I wither slowly in thine arms, / Here at the quiet limit of the world.

I wake out of a dream (*I am on a boat, and the sky has grown dark. Someone stands behind me, touching my arm. As I turn, I see that it is Edgar, only he's younger, much younger, his face more open, eager. He brings my hand halfway to his mouth, and*). A figure shadows my doorway. I am frightened for a moment (*a woman was murdered just last week in Paris, I remember, the details lurid in the papers*), but of course the figure is simply May. Her white nightgown glimmers in the blacks and grays of my room. She eases herself around the embroidery frame, where the white silk floats like a dusky window.

   "Lyddy."

   "Yes, May."

   "May I come into your bed?"

   May has not made such a request in a dozen years at least—

more—although when she was little she often slept in my bed; I knew, whenever we moved to a new house, she would come down the dark hallway and slip into my bed for reassurance, night after night. We moved so often.

I raise the duvet, and May comes in beside me. I give her part of my pillow and touch her face. Wet, is it? I stroke her cheek, and she comes close, her arms around me, her face cradled in the hollow between my shoulder and my breast.

"Are you all right, May?"

I touch her hair. My dream lingers strangely.

Wrapping my arms about her, I feel her delicate shoulder blades, her thin arms. She smells like tobacco smoke, bittersweet, and wine, and something else too, licorice maybe, or sweet, ripe pears. Her lemon cologne is faint now. She seems hot, almost feverish. Her hair brushes against my neck.

"Was the play good, May?"

"*Oui.*"

May moves away from me. She sits on my bed in the dark now, close to me. I can almost see her hair, thick and curling around her shoulders. I cannot see her face.

"I went to Edgar's house afterwards," she adds after a moment. I'm surprised, and can't at first think what to say.

"*Ah bon!* Who went with you?"

"Oh, a few people," May says carefully. "I don't think you know them."

"Did you enjoy their company?"

her arm around his neck, her face joyous

She lies next to me again, on her back. I can see her face gleaming pale in the dark. She's quiet for a long time, and then she says slowly, "Yes. Yes, I did."

I urge myself to be glad for my sister, to grant her her invisible triumph, known only to herself, and, in all quietness, to me. *Good jumping, May, Aleck says, and I say, Be careful.*

May's voice swims out of the dark, thick and strangely harsh. "You won't leave me, will you, Lyddy?"

May brings her face to my shoulder. I feel the heat of her breath on my skin.

"Stay here, don't be sick. I won't be able to live if you become really sick again, and leave me."

"You will, though, May. *Tu vivras.* You'll live as well as you possibly can."

I'm overwhelmed by him.

"I won't be able to paint."

"You will paint. You'll paint gorgeous things."

153

I'll come and see what you do.

"You don't understand, Lyddy. You can't know. I need to know you're in the world. No one else is like you. *Personne.*" She adds, "I always thought I'd have you."

You're the one she loves most in the world.

Then what is death?

"Well, you have me still. *Je suis encore là.*"

I lie awake in the darkness and listen as May's breathing becomes more regular. I hear the city's early-morning sounds: horses on pavement, someone calling to another, a train in the distance. I hold my sister, against the darkness.

viii.

The sky glitters this morning, almost turquoise. Paris shimmers, laid out in a bowl of gay shapes. How strange to be ill on such a day.

Sitting at my embroidery frame after breakfast, posing for May, I gaze again at my wild columbine. I've been able to make only a few stitches. I yearn to fill in my second flower. My back aches, and I cannot feel the thimble on my second finger. I cannot even feel the needle, either above or below the silk ground.

I was sick again this morning, and May looked discouraged as she helped me wash my face and get dressed. I wonder whether this will be May's last picture of me. I think May wonders this too, because there's a new quietness between us. She's intensely focused on her work, and she paints for a long time without a pause.

When Mother comes in for a little while, to read to us, I ask her for "Tithonus," because this poem hovers in my mind today. As she approaches the end, I listen to each word.

> *Yet hold me not for ever in thine East:*
> *How can my nature longer mix with thine?*
> *Coldly thy rosy shadows bathe me, cold*
> *Are all thy lights, and cold my wrinkled feet*
> *Upon thy glimmering thresholds*

"Is Degas coming for tea this week, May?" Mother asks, after she's finished reading.

"Yes, I think so."

> *Release me, and restore me to the ground*

"Is he busy these days?"

"*Oui.* Very."

Thou seest all things, thou wilt see my grave:
Thou wilt renew thy beauty morn by morn.

"Do you think you'll put this one in the Impressionist exhibition, next year?"

"*Je l'espère.*"

Thou wilt renew thy beauty morn by morn;
I earth in earth forget these empty courts,
And thee returning on thy silver wheels.

X.

Two more days of posing, and on the third day, after a long morning, May says, "Time to rest, Lyddy." Her voice sounds oddly gentle. As I move out of my pose, I see May absorbed in putting away her paints.

"The light's changed, Lyddy. We should stop."

May looks at me for a moment, her hand on her hip.

"Would you like to see? I think I almost have it."

I can't imagine May painting another, at least of me, that I could love as well.

In the picture, I bend slightly toward my embroidery, utterly absorbed in what I'm sewing. One can see the silk ground only from underneath, where my hand dissolves into loose brush-strokes, deep pink, white, blue-gray. *What are you embroidering,* I ask myself, *a landscape? a boat?* It could be anything. I'm bent at my labor.

I see now that May's painting creates a kind of memory. Whether or not anyone ever knew me, she will offer a memory of me, for the world to claim. And I see something else: she pictures me as a woman who has had her wishes fulfilled. The day is luminous, the woman's dress a meadow, as she bends to her creation, on her own, desirous simply of what she already has. I yearn to be like this, to have the grace of such satisfaction.

"You've made a whole world, May."

"You like the feeling of it?"

"It's very absorbing."

"I like the way this turned out." May points to the line of the embroidery frame, and I follow her finger right up to the maroon splotch in the middle—her gloves. I think, surely May will be doing more with that. Surely she won't leave it here, marring such a perfect image.

But May says, "I could almost call it done right now."

"Are you sure?"

"*Oui.*"

I gaze at the daubs of paint, especially in the lower half of the painting. Suddenly the whole picture seems to waver. To allow that paint to stay, so unformed—has she ever done this so fully?

"Will you do more with her hand?"

"Maybe not. I like it like that. It's like photographs, Lyddy, when the person moves, or the camera moves, and things blur."

"Yes, I can see that. But in a painting, you have a chance to catch things very still?" I think of the hours I've sat here, my neck aching, precisely to help her paint such stillness.

"But what if things aren't always meant to stay still, Lyddy? Think of it. The world moves, the light changes. Your hand moves, as you embroider."

"But it wasn't moving all the time."

"But if I hadn't been painting you, and you'd simply been embroidering, it would have been."

I feel confused, as if I'm trying to present an important argument to May, but I've lost the thread. *Why not allow incompleteness, change?* I think, and I almost laugh, as I realize how May has met my own thoughts. Even this image of utter satisfaction must show its own artifice, its fragility, its readiness to dissolve into paint, the raggedness of desire.

If May has painted me on an island, then, she has made clear how the sand shifts, how the water works at it, shapes it, dissolves it. When there's lightning, a tree falls, and lizards dart into the underbrush. *And that river of color, there* (I study the maroon, the burgundy—what color is it?): *maybe that's the mud of the island itself, or the blood* (my blood), *the unformed stuff of it. And is it the blood of illness, then, or of life? Or is it of illness and life, both, all rolled together in a terrifying and luscious stream?* It's over my heart, in the picture, almost as if it springs from my heart, or from May's toward me. She knows more about me than I had thought. The color is at once a mistake and a defiant splash: *Here I am, pigment, stuff, the raw material, and what are you going to do about it? It's blood, and desire, and love, and pain, and fury. You can't staunch it. The question is: how to live with it?*

xi.

After lunch, May comes to the threshold of my room, where I am threading a lavender floss to begin Elsie's clover. She buttons her summer coat.

"You're going out?" I ask.

159

"Yes."

She comes in, and quietly takes her burgundy gloves from my embroidery frame.

"To your studio?"

"To a gallery, first, and then to my studio."

I look at her, and she returns my look with her own, teasing, profound.

When she kisses me, I smell her cologne, her freshly washed hair. I catch a glimpse, under her fur collar, of a necklace I have not seen before—pearl, with tiny rubies.

"*Merci*, Lyddy."

"What have I done?"

"You've posed. You've helped me paint." She adds, "I hope you'll be able to pose again soon."

"I hope so too," I say.

Here is what I write. I write it as a letter to May, but I do not wish her to see it, not yet. I put it into my pattern box.

My sister, my soul—when I dissolve, in my heart's blood, I know you will think that you will dissolve too. Your heart will be sore; it will scatter into brush-strokes, fragments, feathers, and you will think you too will vanish. But here is what I wish to tell you. Listen well, May. You will remember me, then, bent over my labor, at my embroidery frame, on a hot June day in Paris, my dress like a field of flowers, my face calm. You will remember me, because you caught my soul in paint. And one day you'll pick up your brush again, and stretch a new canvas, you'll bend to your work again, and the world at your elbow, or crying from the newspapers, or whispering in the shadows near you, will become quieter for a moment, and you will put all these things aside, to make again a world to stand next to that other world, the one we think we know, and you'll hear me whispering, Courage, May, and you'll bend to it, again and again.

    Je t'embrasse,

    Lyddy

Writing this, I feel almost happy. Sometimes one can have a glimpse of the future, and, frightening as it is, it can have in it an element of consolation. Terrible, to imagine a world continuing beyond my own dissolving; yet what if I am a presence for May, and for others too, leaving a trace, like the swath of white light on the top of this embroidery frame? Maybe I should not be so afraid of vanishing, after all.

In the morning, after May has left, I walk into my room to look at Elsie's pillowcase, stretched out still, on my frame, with my designs, yellow, blue, green, purple, lavender. This too is a letter. Poignant but sturdy, this desire to touch another, to reach across an ocean, or a city, or a room. (*Tell me how to live as you do, he said, with such grace. I know nothing about grace.*) My wildflowers look most imperfect. But, slowly, I thread my needle, with a red for the Indian paintbrush, and I begin to sew. Soon, I will create the bee balm too, and then I'll be ready to cut the threads and send this silk field sailing.

I yearn to be simply present in this day, filled for the moment with color and shape, my own hand urging the needle through the silk.

Lydia Cassatt became very ill in the summer of 1881.

She died in Paris on November 7, 1882, of Bright's Disease.

Mary Cassatt painted and created prints for over thirty more years.

She died at her château *in Beaufresne, in 1926.*

I am indebted, in this work of fiction, to the superb scholarship on Mary Cassatt and the Impressionists. I am especially indebted to the work of Robert Herbert, Anne Higonnet, and Nancy Mowll Mathews. The recent exhibition of Cassatt's oeuvre, organized by Judith A. Barter, and the rich accompanying catalogue, *Mary Cassatt: Modern Woman*, have contributed to my understanding of Cassatt's art, family life, and relationship to the world of late nineteenth-century French culture. I wish to thank my research assistant, Jennifer Boittin, for her valuable help.